Seeds Of Suspicion

James Cruickshank

Dedication

This book is dedicated with love to my Daughter in Law, Rachel. Without her doing the formatting and editing my book would never have been born.

Table of Contents

Prologue

It started for him as a normal morning when he walked into the building at his usual time of seven forty-five, this gave him fifteen minutes before he had to see anyone, time to drink the coffee he had bought from the Starbuck's kiosk downstairs, and time for a quick look through the paper.

He had been in his present position for a year, he enjoyed his work, and his colleagues were a great bunch of people.

As he sat down at his desk, he noticed a white envelope addressed to him tucked under the telephone. He opened it and read the note it contained, wondering how it had been delivered.

'Be at the bench at 7 tonight. Please do not let me down, and don't be late.'

It didn't need a signature for him to know who it was from. No names written anywhere had always been their arrangement. The bench was their private rendezvous, so it had to be from her.

It was from a stunning looking young woman, who was gradually yielding to his charm.

She was a real beauty, and almost from the start he had known she was fascinated with him, although up till now, kisses were all she allowed, but he could wait.

It had been very difficult getting to see her alone but eventually he had worked out a plan, that so far was working well. Yet despite his efforts to win her over, he had been unable to bed her, which was his ultimate goal.

She presented a real challenge to him, as the first in a long line of women that had not yet instantly succumbed to his charm, and he was determined to make her another notch on his belt.

Every woman he had ever been out with wanted to be told one thing right from the start. That he loved them, and of course he always said yes. Although love to him, was an unknown quantity. What had love got to do with anything? He certainly desired them, and he pleased them sexually, wasn't that what it was all about?

He had been out on a few dates that had only lasted one night, they had been too easy, he liked a challenge, and that is just what this one was.

A week earlier he had had a couple of days of panic, when he was sure his last girlfriend's husband had twigged that his wife was 'playing away', and with whom. He had even considered leaving town for a while, for his own safety. Her husband was a brute of a man, with quite a reputation for punching first and asking questions afterwards. But thankfully she had convinced him that his suspicions were groundless. But it *had* given him a fright, no doubt about that, now he was letting things cool down a bit with her, concentrating more now with his more recent 'love'.

With her, he had come up with a method of communication that he considered a stroke of genius, it was simple but clever. Whenever she wanted to make contact, she would phone him, let it ring three times and then put the phone down. That would be the signal there was a message waiting for him to collect.

At the rear of the District Commissioner's Office there was bench. Behind this, there was a two-foot length of metal pipe on two uprights, placed there by the Parks Department to support a sagging, ancient and well-loved Jacaranda tree.

The billet-doux, if it could be called that, would be put inside the right-hand end of the cross section to await his collection. And as there had been no signal call on Friday, he could only assume something out of the ordinary must have happened over the weekend for her to alter her routine.

He was completely baffled as to how the envelope had got onto his desk and would ask his secretary when she came in if she knew. As he was thinking this, the lady in question came through the door. He called her over.

"Morning," he said, and asked her.

The only thing she could think of was that it had been given to one of the security guards some time over the weekend, and that they had brought it up; they had keys to all the offices. Her theory satisfied him, and he thanked her. Now there was nothing he could do but wait and see.

He had a rented luxurious bachelor flat, a good job, and was in a relationship with two lovely young married women, things could not be better for him; he was a happy man. He took out the note, read it again, then put it through the shredder.

The day passed painfully slowly for him, and he declined an invitation to go for a light lunch, pleading a queasy tummy, which wasn't too far from the truth?

Promptly at five he picked up his briefcase, called out goodnight and went home. At his flat, he showered and changed into a pair of tan chinos, a pale lemon polo shirt and suede desert boots; a quick squirt of Paco Rabanne on his cheeks and he was out the door.

On reaching the rendezvous he sat down and looked at his watch, he was five minutes early.

At five past seven he got up and walked around to the front of the building, his feelings a jumbled mixture of concern and irritation.

"And she was the one who'd said *don't* be late," he muttered to himself as he looked up and down the deserted street. A couple of cars went past, and he thought, 'I'll leave after the next car.'

As the taillights of the third car disappeared into the distance he walked back to the bench. She still had not arrived.

He was just about to sit down when an arm was wrapped around his throat from behind in a choke hold, and he was pulled violently backwards. His spine made sudden and very painful contact with the back of the bench. He gave a cry of pain, and tried to shout, but the pressure on his throat made that impossible. He reached back with both hands, desperately trying to pull the arm away from his neck; but it was a vice like grip cutting off his blood supply. His head began to spin, his arms fell to his side, and as darkness overtook him, his last thoughts were...the beast!

He regained consciousness slowly. Totally disoriented, his head was pounding, and his throat felt as if it had been crushed.

He was lying on his back on a cold stone floor, looking up at what appeared to be a metal grill. He looked at his watch, there was nothing on his wrist. He then realised he was completely naked, even his shoes had gone.

It must have been around six in the morning as the sky was just beginning to lighten and he could now see his surroundings. The room he was in was about seven feet square, with a floor sloping to his right, and down towards the far corner, where he could see the opening of a drain about ten inches across. He looked to his left, there was a large steel pipe coming from the wall. It branched out into three smaller pipes, each with a wheeled valve at the top. On the wall to his right there were steel rungs set into the brickwork, leading up to what he could now clearly see was a heavy metal grill set into, and forming about a quarter of the ceiling. 'Where the hell was he?'

Then he remembered watching a television documentary program recently, about the old pipeline, that brought water from some dam or other to ease the City's serious water problem; and that a new pipeline was due to be built.

It described the chambers that had been installed at intervals along it, containing valves, which could be opened and closed, if repairs were necessary.

There was one more thing they had spoken about, something to do with inspection; for the life of him he could not think what; but this was definitely one of those chambers.

Realisation as to where he was made him panic. Was he just going to be left here to die; he wracked his brains trying to work out who had brought him here, and why?

As if a light bulb had suddenly gone off in his head his mind screamed at him.

"My God, it must be Desirée's husband! He's found out about us; but why hadn't the stupid bitch warned me?'"

He had not moved since regaining consciousness, and when he tried to sit up, he found he was feeling very weak. His arms and legs were numb and bruised, and it took nearly ten minutes of gradually easing himself up, before he was able to stand.

There was still something about the chambers, with their grills and locks and valves niggling at his mind. Then it came to him in a flash. The TV commentator had mentioned that the grills were securely padlocked for security reasons, that the chambers were visited every fortnight, and strict records were made each time. 'That was it… the inspections!'

He looked frantically around the room. 'Did they keep the inspection sheet here, or back in their office?' Hope surged in his chest as he saw a chart hanging by a string from one of the valves, that must be it. He shuffled across to look. This would show when the next inspection was due.

Hope died as quickly as it had been born. The last date was shown as 25/6, and presuming this was his first day here, they had been inspected the day before.

He slumped onto the floor, lifted his head, and screamed. *"How the hell am I going to get out, I will be dead long before the next inspection?"*

He began to sob, knowing it would be no use shouting, nobody would be able to hear him, as the chambers were all set way back from the road.

Two cold miserable days and nights had passed, and apart from bird calls, the only sound he heard in all that time was the rumble of far distant traffic. His fingers were bleeding, and two of his nails had ripped off where he had tried to shut off one of the valves. Over the years it had accumulated quite a bit of rust, but he was too weak to close it. He had reasoned that if he were able to close even one of them, someone would come to investigate the problem; but they were all seized up.

Despite knowing it was pointless, he had continued calling for help. His shouts had eventually become almost mindless screaming, until with a tongue that felt like a piece of leather, and lips that cracked and bled every time he opened his mouth, even the screams had eventually become the occasional desperate croak.

At dawn on the third day, he had given up all hope and was prepared to die. He couldn't think properly and was beginning to hallucinate. He kept trying to fathom out why he was there, but his thought processes were too damaged by lack of food and water. Slowly he began to drift into the world of endless darkness, but he no longer cared, his mind and body had almost given up.

The crash of the grill being thrown open jolted him back to semi reality. He next became aware of a silent figure standing over him. He felt his shoulders being raised, then blessed nectar, as warm water was dribbled into his mouth. He desperately wanted to gulp it down to fill himself until he burst, but it was only a dribble. He tried unsuccessfully to reach up and hold the bottle to his mouth, but he was too weak. After a few minutes of frantically lapping at the life-giving water, his tongue and mouth felt more normal. He snatched up the sandwiches he was offered and devoured them in seconds.

His 'rescuer' laid him back onto the floor and stood there looking down at him, still not having spoken a word, and he was just able to manage a feeble.

"Hello."

He could now make out the shape of a man, and gradually the man's features become recognizable. It suddenly felt as if a cold hand had squeezed his heart. He knew this was not a rescue after all,   and   that   hell   was   about   to   begin.

Chapter One

The day had ended well for Neil Owens; over lunch he had successfully negotiated with the City Council for the construction of a new water main, from the Sasamua dam in the Highlands to Nairobi, which would increase the much-needed supply by 100%. The pipeline currently in use had been built when his father owned the company ten years ago.

He had inherited the business after his parents had been killed in a light plane crash, shortly after his 21st birthday, leaving him the richest and most sought-after bachelor in the Colony.

The hundreds of new residences with thirsty owners and gardens springing up around the city almost daily, made the old supply totally inadequate; and despite the enormous cost, it *had* to be built.

It would take four years to complete, and Neil had managed to pull off the deal at a price that made the City Fathers, very pleased with him. He smiled to himself as he thought of what he would buy with the cheque he knew was coming. It would get him the Fire Red Porsche that had been sitting in the Motor Mart showroom for the last month, just waiting for him to come along.

Neil was a fourth generation Kenyan, who ran his own business. Born in Nairobi where he had always lived. His home was a luxurious four-bedroom house, sited on three acres in Muthaiga, the most affluent suburb of the city.

You had to be at least a millionaire to buy there now, but Neil's great-great grandfather had purchased 100 acres, in the late 1800's, when nobody wanted it, for a few shillings an acre.

Over the following years the family had gradually sold off the land as two acre building plots; except for their plot, which was three acres.

For five years Neil had juggled his life between getting his Master of Science degree in Ground Hydrology, from Cape Town University, and an acceptable social life. How he had ever managed to do that, he would never know, but he had, and was now well respected in his chosen field.

Aged twenty-six he had finally given up bachelorhood and had married a twenty-one-year-old fiery red head by the name of Fiona, the daughter of Duncan and Moira McDonald.

Neil considered Fiona one of the most beautiful women he had ever seen. She was a petite five foot four and weighed exactly one hundred and twelve pounds. She had green eyes the colour of jade that could drown the strongest of swimmers in a sea of mystique, if he looked too deeply into them.

Many a local lad had set his cap at her, but it was Neil who had finally captured her heart. They were ideally suited, with most of the important things in life a common interest, and it was obvious to everyone they were very much in love.

Her father was an extremely wealthy coffee farmer, and Neil's friends took great delight in teasing him, saying 'money certainly does get money', and Neil had to agree.

At six foot two inches and weighing a solid one hundred and ninety-five pounds, Neil was a fine figure of a man. His dark brown, almost black hair was always neatly trimmed, and his hazel eyes could sometimes be soft and romantic, as when he looked at Fiona. But when someone, or something, seriously upset him, they became as hard as agate, with the unmistakably clear message, 'you're treading on dangerous ground.'

He kept in shape by training twice weekly at his club gym, followed by fifty fast lengths of their international size swimming pool. He played rugby as prop for the Old Cambrian's fifteen, and was considered by all, a real asset to the team.

His physique, best displayed when in a swimming costume, brought many looks of longing and admiration from women of all ages when seeing him on the beach or at the pool. Fiona never knew whether to be proud or cross when she saw their reaction. She guessed it was really a mixture of both.

And it was not only the women that took note of his body, many men also gave it envious looks, wishing they were like him. But despite this, Neil had not a conceited bone in his body, which was just one of the many reasons that Fiona adored him.

Altogether he was considered by all who knew him, as a most presentable and honourable man. Friends he considered a very precious commodity, and the maxim, 'a friend in need is a friend indeed,' was something he truly believed in. He would do anything to help a friend, and in return he expected the same.

Not only had he all the money he would ever need, and only worked because he loved his job, but his wife was one of the prettiest and most vivacious young women in the city. To add to his happiness, he was captain of the prestigious Muthaiga Golf Club, a position he had held for two years.

He felt contentment bubbling out of him as he sat looking at the completed contract for the new work on his desk. Life just could not get better.

He looked over at the single photograph on his desk, it was of Fiona taken on their honeymoon on Mahé by the hotel photographer; it really captured both her spirit and her beauty. Marrying her was without a doubt the best thing that had ever happened to him.

He remembered the night they had both stood nervously in her parent's lounge, with him waiting sweaty palmed to tell them they had become engaged and wished to get married in three months time on her birthday.

Neil thought he was going to pass out with relief on hearing that Duncan and Moira McDonald fully approved of their only daughter's choice and wished them both happiness for the future.

After much input from Moira, they unanimously decided to forgo the traditional engagement party, and settled for dinner and drinks for the four of them at Tors Hotel.

Back at the McDonalds, Moira whisked Fiona away to her bedroom to explain the arrangements she wanted to make for the wedding, leaving Duncan to casually quiz Neil on his financial position, of which he was already aware.

A month before the wedding day, Fiona's father the archetypal canny Scot, nearly had a fit when Moira informed him that she was taking Fiona to Paris to purchase her wedding dress and trousseau, and of course her own outfit. But despite his protestations that there were perfectly good dress shops in Nairobi, and that she did not need to go all the way to Paris, Moira was adamant that that was where they were going.

Duncan McDonald, although one of the richest men in Kenya was also well know as someone who watched his pennies. Basically very down to earth, a man who could not abide unnecessary frills and fancies, and despite his wife's never-ending protestations, he had his own little foible; rolling his own cigarettes.

It was painful enough for her to watch when he rolled them at home, but whenever they were out with friends or had guests, as soon as the little green tin, and that disgusting little gadget he used to make them were produced, she would beat a hasty retreat to the powder room, unable to cope with the acute bout of embarrassment this caused her.

Watching him rolling the cigarettes was bad enough, but when he ran his tongue along the paper to wet it, that was too much. Her rapid departure was guaranteed to bring a smile to the faces of their friends; they were well used to it and found the whole scenario amusing. Moira however, even after twenty-three years of marriage, could not, and would not accept it as acceptable social behaviour.

This was not to be Fiona's first, trip to Paris. Her parents had taken her there one summer when she was ten, but Paris seen through the eyes of a child, was not the Paris as seen by those of a mature young woman. Still, even aged ten she had liked Paris so much she chose to take French at school, and now spoke the language as if born there. She was very excited at the prospect of the trip, but the thought of being away from Neil for the first time since they had met, was taking the edge off it just a little.

Their hotel was in the centre of Paris, accessible to all the best stores, and for the first two days all they did was shop. Fiona was overwhelmed by the choice and quality of the clothing and jewellery compared to Nairobi, and the two of them spent a lot of money.

One night they went to a show at the Moulin Rouge. It was absolutely breath taking, and both said how much Duncan and Neil would have enjoyed it.

Day three they planned to do some sight seeing, and after visiting Notre Dame and the Sacre Coeur found themselves in

4

Montmartre. It was fascinating, with art shops on every side, and artists making sketches and paintings of passers-by everywhere.

They wandered around for a while going from one artist to another comparing their work. Fiona particularly liked the pastel likenesses and wanted to take one back as a present for Neil. She finally decided on an elderly gentleman who was very much in demand and had to wait for an hour before he could begin, but it was well worth the wait.

He was very talented and had captured Fiona's beauty and independent spirit perfectly. He insisted on spraying the drawing with an aerosol of quick drying lacquer before giving it to her, explaining that it would prevent the colours smudging, he then carefully rolled the drawing, tied it with a red ribbon, and before handing it over, took her hand and kissed it.

"It was indeed a pleasure and an honour Mademoiselle."

Fiona thanked him, looked at her watch and said to Moira.

"Let's find a nice little restaurant and have lunch."

Just then Fiona felt a tug at her handbag, she turned to see a youth running away with her purse in his hand. She shouted and he looked back at her, then ran straight into a young man who had stepped out of a shop. He had obviously seen what had happened because he caught hold of the boy's arm, and despite his wild struggles did not let go.

The saying that you can never find a policeman when you want one, was not quite true that day, because at that moment, round the corner came two gendarmes, who on seeing the struggle went over to investigate. The youth had now stopped trying to break loose and stood quietly as the young man spoke to one of the gendarmes. He pointed to Fiona and then nodded his head, obviously agreeing to something the policeman had said to him.

He came over to Fiona, and in perfect English with a voice that reminded her of the French singer Sacha Distel introduced himself.

"Mademoiselle, my name is Pascal Perigeux. I believe this is yours," he said, and handed her the purse.

Fiona wondered how he knew to address her in English, and then remembered that some French friends of hers had once told her, that no matter how the English dressed when in France, without even hearing them speak, they knew at a glance that they were English.

Fiona thanked him and they were just about to walk away when he addressed them again.

"Unfortunately, Mademoiselle, the police require us to attend the police station and make a statement so the boy can be charged."

"I don't really want to make a fuss," Fiona said, "we are only here for another day, and they may want us to go to court."

"Have no fear of that. In France, your statement and mine will be sufficient evidence for the judge."

Pascal showed them the way to the police station, which was just around the corner, and after writing and signing their statements, Moira and Fiona waited outside for Pascal, just to say thank you and goodbye, but he would have none of it.

"Thank you…yes…but goodbye. No! I wish to show you that not all Frenchmen are like that thief, may I offer you and your sister lunch?"

"Oh no Monsieur," Fiona said blushing furiously, "We are not sisters, this is my mother, Moira MacDonald, and my name is Fiona."

Fiona looked at her mother, suddenly seeing her in a completely different light, Moira had married Duncan as a very young girl, and now even at forty-two, was an extremely attractive woman, she looked nowhere near her age, and Fiona could see that her mother wanted her to accept the invitation.

"You don't have to do that, but thank you, lunch would be most welcome. We were just about to try and find somewhere to eat when this happened."

"Wonderful," he said. "I have just the place for us."

The restaurant he had chosen for them was called Ma Maison. It was small, softly lit and very homely, the owner acting as both chef ad barman, with his wife and daughter as cashier and waitress.

They spent a very pleasant hour dining on moule-frites and white wine, and during the meal, Pascal told them he was a professor at the Sorbonne and had lived in Paris all his life.

Pascal flirted outrageously with Moira, and Fiona was not quite sure whether she was feeling outraged at this virtual stranger coming on to her mother, or annoyed that it was not her he was

6

paying so much attention to. She decided it was neither, and actually enjoyed watching her mother's reaction to his flattery.

He enquired as to how they planned to spend their last day in Paris, and when told they would like to visit the Eiffel Tower, he said he would very much like to accompany them as their guide.

Before Fiona had a chance to accept his offer, Moira said that would be wonderful. He asked the name of their hotel and arranged to collect them the next day at twelve. Moira blushed as he took her hand and kissed it, saying.

"Until tomorrow." He then kissed Fiona's hand, and said the same to her, before turning and walking away.

"What a dream," Moira said wistfully, "just wait until I tell your father he nearly lost me to a Frenchman…but on second thoughts, maybe I won't."

Fiona looked at her mother and they both burst out laughing at the same time. Passers-by eyed them with amusement as mother and daughter joined hands and did a little 'ring a ring of roses' dance calling out.

"*Until tomorrow.*"

Pascal was already waiting for them when they came out of the hotel, and ushered them quickly into his car, indicating with his head the traffic policeman making his way towards them. As he drove away, he asked.

"Have you been on the Seine yet?"

Fiona shook her head.

"In that case, first we shall do that, to visit Paris and not go on the Seine is a sin, then after that, the Eiffel Tower. The best time for the tower is about one hour before dusk, then you will see Paris at her best…but first the Seine."

Pascal chose what he considered the best river launch, and after a superb lunch onboard, they spent the next two hours serenely cruising along the Seine for a mile or so, first up one side on then back down the other, entertained by a group of very talented youngsters with guitars and keyboard. Moira and Fiona agreed with Pascal that it would indeed have been a tragedy to have missed out on the excursion.

Judging by the number of people queuing for the lifts, the Eiffel tower was an extremely popular place, but not only with tourists; Fiona was surprised at the number of people speaking French.

While they waited for Pascal to get their tickets, Fiona and Moira read the information about the tower. It was completed in 1889, and until 1939, with a height of 300 metres it was the tallest structure in the world.

Getting to the top of the tower entailed travelling in different lifts because of the tower's widespread base, and somehow the three of them always seemed to end up packed into the centre of each lift, and with so many people around them they saw virtually nothing until they finally reached the top level.

The view from there was magnificent, but Pascal assured them it was nothing to what it would be later. He looked at his watch.

"Come, there is plenty of time for viewing later, let's go into the bar and have a drink or two."

They found a table by a window, and Moira insisted on ordering and paying for a bottle of champagne.

She must have thought that as she was paying for it, it entitled her to have the lion's share, and after her second glass her eyes were sparkling; now she was the one doing the flirting.

She reached across the table and took Pascal's hand.

"I think Pascal Perigeux sounds so romantic," she sighed.

Pascal looked at her and smiled.

"Believe me Moira, when I was a boy, I hated my name."

Moira let go of his hand and leant back.

"Why on earth would you do that Pascal? I think Pascal is a lovely name."

"When I was fifteen I was small for my age, and all the kids used to…" he paused as if he was reconsidering telling them the rest. "They used to call by a nick name that I hated." His face was now flushed.

"Well!" Moira said, "what *was* your nick name? It can't be worse than some of the ones I've had."

Pascal laughed with embarrassment.

"They called me 'little PeePee'…you know…Pascal Perigeux…my initials."

8

Moira had been taking a sip of champagne, and nearly choked on it when she heard this. She looked at Fiona and they both began to laugh.

A very embarrassed Pascal watched them, then realising they were laughing with him and not at him, he joined in; they all reached across the table and clasped hands.

As the sun sank closer to the horizon and the sky grew darker, the whole world around them began to twinkle, with lights appearing as if from nowhere. Streetlights, house lights, traffic lights, multi coloured flashing neon signs, car head lights and taillights, and even in the sky, navigation lights from aeroplanes going to, and coming from Orly airport; it truly was a magical time.

Neither of the two women had thought to bring coats with them, and Moira was beginning to feel the chill of evening. Pascal noticed this.

"Unfortunately ladies, I have a pre arranged appointment that I must keep this evening, so perhaps now would be a good time to for us to leave."

Moira and Fiona took one more turn around the observation platform, trying to fix the sight of Paris stretching from horizon to horizon firmly in their memories, before heading for the lift.

Pascal drove them back to the hotel and walked with them to the front door. He kissed each of them in turn, saying how much he had enjoyed their company, and as he got into the car he called out.

"Do not forget, if ever you return to Paris, my number is in the book."

With a sharp double toot on the horn, he pulled out into the traffic, and disappeared into the night.

Chapter Two

Seated in the back of Duncan's Bentley Neil could see that Fiona was excited, and had something on her mind, but he could not think why or what. They had not even got halfway home from the airport, when unable to contain her excitement any longer, she handed him a small package; but not before tearing off the wrapping paper.

"It's just a little thing, from me to you...your wedding gift," she said nervously, "I hope you like it...it's from Cartier."

Moira turned around and asked what it was?

"Just wait mum, it's Neil's surprise, not yours

Neil smiled at her and hoped she would never change. Fiona loved getting presents, but always got far more pleasure in giving them. He took the small dark blue velvet covered box she was holding out to him and opened it. What he saw made his eyebrows lift, a gesture she immediately picked up on, causing her to smile.

Nestling on a bed of black silk was a pair of cuff links. Not just ordinary cuff links, but works of art. They were thumbnail sized replicas of a lion's head made from 9ct gold, each with two small diamonds for the eyes. Neil was speechless.

"You do like them don't you Neil?" she asked, her voice quivering with apprehension.

Neil looked up at her, with moist eyes.

"Like them! Like does not even come close to explain what I think of them. This must be the most fantastic present I have ever been given. Thank you, my darling."

Fiona breathed a sigh of relief.

"I know I shouldn't have given you it now, but I can always get you something else to give you on the day, if you would like."

That did not require a reply and Neil smiled to himself, knowing that whatever she bought, and whenever she bought it, she would give it to him the same day. His birthday and Christmas presents always came early.

Their wedding was to take place in St Andrews, the Scots Kirk at the foot of Hospital hill, with the reception for one hundred guests at the Norfolk Hotel.

On the big day, Neil, and Trevor his best man, arrived at the church half an hour before the ceremony was due to begin, they were now standing at the front of the church nervously awaiting the bride's arrival.

With ten minutes to go, Neil said.

"Let's go inside", she will be here any minute now."

The church was already bursting at the seams with the guests anxiously waiting for their first glimpse of the bride, and because of the sheer number of people who could not possibly, according to Moira, be left off the list, there were a few obviously disappointed late comers standing outside; the women all wearing different hats and dresses, but all with the same peevish look on their faces.

Duncan, as father of the bride, and therefore responsible for paying for it all, had wanted a small ceremony and dinner at their home, but his suggestion had crashed and died in flames, shot down by Moira's barrage of anger.

For the umpteenth time since their arrival, Neil asked Trevor if he was sure he had remembered to bring the ring.

"If you ask me that one more time, I am going to give you the damn thing and go home, then you can be groom, and best man,"

With only a few minutes to go before Fiona's arrival, Neil was beginning to get the expected bridegroom's jitters. 'Will the car break down, has she changed her mind, did he look alright…had Trevor really brought the ring?'

He turned to his friend to speak and changed his mind on seeing the look on Trevor's face.

Neil had no cause to worry as to whether Fiona had changed her mind about marrying him. Although only twenty-one, she had had her fair share of boyfriends, and knew without a shadow of doubt that Neil was the man for her.

Moira looked at her future son in law and gave a slight nod of approval. Neil's suit was made of pale grey lightweight cashmere. Tailored to perfection it showed off his physique perfectly. His suit was complemented by a cream silk shirt from Paris, fastened at the wrists with his lion head cuff links; his tie was pale lilac raw silk

12

bought especially to please Fiona, as it was one of her favourite colours. He was the epitome of elegance.

Moira had wanted the full works for her only daughter's wedding, with the men all dressed up in morning suits. Neil had been adamantly against the idea, and thankfully he was supported by Fiona, and Duncan, who wanted to wear his full highland dress, currently stowed away with mothballs in the attic.

"You wouldn't be able to bury me in one of those outfits," Neil had told Moira, and she could not persuade him to change his mind, which she tried to do every time they met.

Each time while she was yammering on, Neil filled his mind with images of other weddings he had attended in the past, where the men, dressed in hired clothes, looked as if their outfits had been thrown at them, and they had grabbed whatever they could, all ending up with trousers three inches too long, tight jackets, and hats, that if they didn't have ears, would be down over their eyes.

The organ suddenly began to play the Wedding March, quietening the impatient murmuring of the guests, who immediately turned their heads towards the church entrance, each one wanting to be the first to see the bride.

Neil did not know if the groom was expected to stay facing the altar until the bride was at his side, or if he should be watching her walk down the aisle. He chose the latter.

Duncan looked splendid, dressed in his Highland regalia, the kilt swinging jauntily with each slow step. A man proud of his Scottish heritage taking his beautiful daughter to marry the man he knew would be a husband and son in law that anyone could wish for.

As he came down the aisle with Fiona clinging to his arm Neil could hardly believe his eyes. He had been hoping that Fiona's dress was her choice and not Moira's, but as soon as he saw her his concern disappeared.

Fiona was one of those truly beautiful women that looked stunning in whatever they wore. He had always told her that she would look good even if she was covered in mud, but today she was out of this world. Just looking at her left him speechless. With the sun streaming through the stained-glass windows behind her, the image that came to his mind was, a goddess, dressed by angels.

Her dress must have been designed and put together by an expert. It was made of cream wild silk and studded all over with miniature freshwater pearls. It had a fashionably low-cut bodice and emphasised a waistline that most women would die for, with the full skirt gently brushing along the floor as she walked.

To Moira's dismay, Fiona had chosen not to have either a veil or a train, which suited Neil, he wanted everyone to see just how beautiful she was.

Fiona's naturally red hair had been braided and swept up in the French style and crowned with a halo of mock orange blossom.

Two young McDonald girl cousins, identical twins, walked behind Fiona. They were her uncle's grandchildren and had both inherited the McDonald red hair, dressed identically in long cream dresses, both a picture of innocence.

Fiona's bouquet was an arrangement of orchids, with their colours complementing her red hair, green eyes, and cream dress. They had been flown in the day before from Taiwan, an expense which must have caused Duncan's wallet to groan. The bouquet completed the picture that was eliciting mixed sighs of both admiration and envy from the female guests.

The ceremony went by in what was almost a blur to Neil. He was so nervous Trevor had to prompt him to say.

"I do," and his hands were shaking so much he almost dropped the ring. Before he fully realised it, he was a married man, and found himself with his wife on the church steps, being photographed.

After the photo session Fiona was faced by a group of eager eyed hopefuls, all waiting for her to throw the bouquet over her shoulder; she turned and threw it.

One young woman more athletically built than the others leaped up and snatched it out of the air. She turned with a shriek of triumph and displayed her prize to the young man with her, who then began backing away with an apprehensive look on his face.

Moira had arranged for a changing room at the hotel for the young couple, and halfway through a very noisy reception, and after listening to a tearful Duncan, with a few single malts under his sporran, telling them all for the third time, how much he was going to miss his lovely daughter, but how proud he was to have gained a

14

son, Neil and Fiona quietly slipped away to change into their travelling clothes.

The taxi that had been booked and paid for by the hotel manager with his compliments, took them out to Nairobi International Airport, where they boarded the afternoon flight on a Kenya Airways 737, bound for their honeymoon destination, Mahé in the Seychelles Islands.

Chapter Three

The afternoon flight to Mahé proved to be boring, with a flight time too short to enjoy a good film, and not long enough to have a good sleep.

They were dozing when the captain called attention to the fact that the first of the islands were now in sight on either side of the cabin.

Neil listened as the captain explained that the Seychelles was an archipelago of over one hundred islands, stretching for one thousand miles, and that their destination Mahé, was the largest, measuring fifty - seven square miles.

The touch down at Mahé International was a little bumpy due to a crosswind, and Neil's arm felt as if it was a rottweiler hanging onto it, not the nervous wreck sitting next to him, Fiona hated flying at the best of times, but especially the landing.

With the island keen to encourage tourism, they found the airport customs and immigration officers very friendly, and compared to their own airport, both fast and efficient.

They were booked into the Coco de Mer, a luxury five-star hotel, south of Anse Royale. It had been recommended by friends at their club, and as they pulled up at the front of the hotel in their courtesy car, they knew that going by appearance and setting alone, they had made the right choice. Situated on the eastern side of Mahé right on the beach, with nothing between it and the Indian Ocean made it perfect. Even the name, Coco de Mer sounded romantically suitable for a honeymoon.

Their booking had been made by telephone, and Neil had dealt personally with the manager, a jovial sounding man; with his accent, and the name Antoine Laporte, Neil had guessed that he was of French extraction.

A small immaculately dressed man of about forty wearing a cream light weight suit, with a crimson magnolia in his buttonhole came out from the hotel foyer to meet them. His outstretched hand and beaming smile were a good indication that they were about to receive a warm welcome.

His voice and image matched the impression that Neil had formed in his mind. He smiled as the man shook his hand and then kissed Fiona's.

"Bon soir Monsieur et Madame Owens," he said in the sing song cadence so typical of the islands, and the sound of his voice tickled the hairs on the back of Fiona's neck.

"My name is Antoine Laporte. I am the manager and owner. May I welcome you to the Coco de Mer the finest hotel in all of the islands?"

He ushered them into the hotel, while snapping his fingers impatiently at the porters struggling manfully with Fiona's suitcases, most of which had travelled as excess baggage, and at rather an *excess* charge Neil had thought.

He escorted them to the front desk to complete the check-in formalities, and then took them up in the lift to their apartment. On reaching their front door, Fiona noticed straight away that their suite was named Queen of the Night and remarked on it.

The manager explained that their apartment was one of four that occupied the top floor of the hotel and unlike the other accommodation which all had numbers, the individual apartments were identified by names of flowers, the two to the rear were *Hibiscus* and *Magnolia,* the more in demand seaward facing apartments, *Frangipani,* and theirs *Queen of the night*.

He unlocked the door and stood aside to let them enter.

"Please Monsieur Owens…Madame, if there is anything I can do to make your stay with us more than pleasant, do not hesitate to call me," he said following them into the room.

Neil felt sorry for the three sweat soaked porters it had taken to bring up what was mainly Fiona's luggage as the manager herded them quickly into the bedroom to deposit the bags, and then shooed them straight out the front door before Neil could give them a more than a well-earned tip.

As the manager turned to leave, he again assured them that the hotel really valued their patronage, saying.

"Mersi, pas en bon letan sesel." On seeing the puzzled look on Neil's face, he quickly explained "It is Kreol, or as you would know it, Creole, the patois of the islands. It means thank you, have an enjoyable stay in the Seychelles."

He said goodbye again, but before leaving the room, asked them to please call him Antoine.

"That's fine Antoine," Neil replied, "as long it's Neil and Fiona to you."

Antoine smiled, and bowed.

"It is an honour."

"Just one thing before you go Antoine. I would like to do some deep-sea fishing, could you make some enquiries for me please?"

"Most certainly. Bonne Nuit. Neil…Fiona."

Fiona was really amused by the whole thing and burst out laughing after the door closed.

"He is such a sweet little man, I'm sure he thinks you are a billionaire."

"He is very professional," Neil said in the manager's defence, "and it's certainly nice to meet one that is for a change, I'm sure he treats all his guests that way. And he certainly likes you. I saw the way he kissed your hand. No wonder you enjoyed your trip to Paris so much if he is an example of what they are like over there."

The first thing they noticed in the lounge was a bouquet of flowers, and a large bowl of fruit; next to it was a silver bucket full to the brim with ice from which protruded the neck of a bottle of Dom Perignon and two crystal flutes. There was also a card. 'With the compliments of the hotel.'

Adjoining the lounge which was enormous was the bedroom, dominated by the biggest bed they had ever seen. An en suite bathroom with a walk-in shower, bath, hot tub, and to Fiona's delight, twin wash hand basins.

The apartment was unbelievable. It was obvious that no expense had been spared in the decorating and furnishing, with the guest's comfort uppermost in the hotel designer's mind.

They had thought of everything, from the bar which ran along part of one wall, stocked with bottles of just about every drink a thirsty guest could desire, to the unique wall facing the sea which took up the whole length of the lounge. It was made of floor to ceiling storm proof glass half of which was designed to slide back electronically, with the same remote control that opened and closed the curtains.

The sliding windows allowed them out onto a spacious balcony which stretched from one end of the apartment to the other.

More than adequately equipped with comfortably padded sun beds complete with individual umbrellas and a scattering of small tables, it was an ideal place to lie back and enjoy the morning sun.

The view was unbelievable with a horizon so clear they could actually see the curvature of the earth.

One half of the balcony was protected from the elements by more storm proof glass windows just in case the wind was a bit too strong, and there was a notice on the wall, asking guests to 'kindly move all the furniture behind the glass when the weather is inclement, especially the umbrellas.'

Neil and Fiona saw no reason to be typical honeymooners, with the usual tearing off clothes and rushing into the bedroom. They had been lovers for long enough for them to know each other's likes and dislikes in the bedroom and had reached a more than satisfactory stage in their love making.

While Fiona went through to the bathroom to do her hair Neil explored the apartment and there was a lot of it to explore.

Like a young boy, he opened and closed the sliding doors so many times that an exasperated Fiona finally came through from the bedroom and shouted at him.

"If you don't stop playing with those bloody windows right now, I'm going to throw you off the balcony!"

Neil explained that as an engineer he was not 'playing' but was interested in the mechanics of it, and changed the subject by asking if she would rather eat in the dining room or have room service bring something up?

"Something here I think darling, I don't really feel like dressing up on our first evening. You order something nice."

Neil phoned room service, placed his order, and called through to the bedroom.

"Half on hour darling, okay?" There was no reply, so he took that as a yes.

Neil was absolutely fascinated with the entertainment system in the room, which comprised of a TV and a built in Hi Fi record player with speakers around the room.

While Fiona was in the bedroom unpacking, he switched the television on and began playing with the remote control; a notice on the side of the set informed him that with the three-metre dish on the roof of the hotel they were able to receive hundreds of channels from all over the world.

A knock on the door interrupted his play and reluctantly he went to answer it. He opened the door to find a well laden trolley waiting to be wheeled in, and surprise, surprise, there were the same three porters that had brought up their luggage now all smartly dressed as waiters. They trooped into the room, each one trying to make it look as if he was the only one pushing it.

A picture flashed into Neil's mind of the old classic comedians, The Three Stooges and he struggled to keep a straight face. This time they left the room much happier than they had earlier, each one with a fifty rupee note tucked away in their back pocket.

Fiona came into the room and began lifting the covers to see what he had ordered.

"Whatever it is it smells wonderful. I'm starving," she said, with her mouth half full, nibbling away at the finger sized Lourenço Marques prawn.

Neil had ordered Tiger prawns with a piri piri garlic sauce on a bed of wild rice, with a Caesar Salad on the side. Piri piri was a hot sauce made from a variety of spices, but mainly very hot chillies. For dessert he had chosen Pear Tartare with a Cointreau double cream topping.

Fiona slapped Neil playfully on the wrist.

"*Don't* dip your roll in the piri sauce Neil that's disgusting!" She tilted her head to one side and thought for a moment. "Let's leave the champagne until a little later shall we? I think I rather fancy a coffee."

After what really had been a superb meal, Neil stretched out on the settee, while Fiona went over to the bar to make coffee.

"You aren't going to believe this Neil, but we actually have Jamaican Blue Mountain here."

21

"For what all this is going to cost us I should damn well think so, and anyway nothing is too good for you my darling."

The coffee certainly lived up to its reputation and they each had a second cup, with Fiona beginning to get more and more irritated with Neil as he sat next to her flicking repeatedly through the channels on the TV.

"I know there are supposed to be a couple of hundred channels darling. But do you really want to check everyone of them out on our first evening here?"

"Sorry, I'll switch it off."

"No you stay and have fun I'm going to shower and change, just don't get too engrossed in whatever you finally decide to watch."

Neil was so captivated with his new toys that he had momentarily forgotten they were on their honeymoon. That is until his nose twitched, and the familiar scent of Hawaiian Ginger tickled his nostrils; he looked behind him. Across the room he saw Fiona wearing a negligee that was so sheer it was almost invisible.

She was leaning in a nonchalant pose with one shoulder against the doorway to the bedroom looking extremely seductive. She beckoned to him slowly with one finger and nodded her head towards the bed.

"You go and shower, I'll open the champagne."

Neil must have broken the world record in the 'quickest shower event for men', and the flutes of champagne still had beads of condensation on them when he came back into the lounge. She laughed when she saw that he had wrapped the gaily coloured cotton kikoi he had bought from the market in Stewart Street the week before, tightly around his waist. He felt a little self-conscious at her laughter.

"Would you rather I took it off?"

"Oh yes" she said, laughing again. "Definitely…But not just yet, let's see off this bottle of champagne first."

Neil picked up the two glasses and handed one to her as she asked.

"Be an angel and get me my kimono from the bedroom would you, Neil it's chillier than I thought."

22

He came back and draped the kimono around her shoulders. She slipped her arms through the sleeves and once she had fastened the belt they went out onto the balcony.

Fiona leant against the balcony rail staring out to sea. Neil came up behind her, leant forward and kissed the back of her neck. She gave a quiet *Hmmm* of pleasure and leant back into his body and as always when he made bodily contact with her, he felt himself becoming aroused. He put his head down towards hers and took in deep breath. The perfume she was wearing always turned him on, not that he needed it now, not with her pressed up against him.

Women were strange he thought; only a few minutes ago she had said she was feeling a bit cold, but the parts of her that were now up against him were anything but cold. In fact it felt as if she was running a fever.

Neil felt blood rushing to his brain and his ears were buzzing. He vaguely heard Fiona saying something to him and shook his head to clear it.

"Sorry darling, what was that you said?"

"I said…look out there at that huge ship, I wonder where it's going?"

Neil looked over her shoulder, he could see the ship and it *was* big. Not only was it big, but it was showing enough lights to light up a small sized town. He estimated that it was about a mile offshore and heading south; every now and again they could hear an orchestra playing; the sound carried to them by the slight onshore breeze.

"They certainly seem to be having a good time probably a cruise ship on its way to Mauritius, I wouldn't mind being on her."

Fiona dug him sharply in the ribs.

"It had better be with me, lover."

As they watched the ship moving slowly from left to right, it suddenly disappeared.

"They've switched off all the lights, I wonder why?"

She had no sooner said that when two white rockets burst high in the sky above the ship, followed immediately by dozens of different coloured rockets. It was strange seeing the great globes of multi coloured fire exploding silently in the night sky, followed a

23

couple of heart beats later by the explosions. Then suddenly all its lights came back on again.

"I wonder what all that was about?" Neil said. "Maybe they had someone really important on board, celebrating their birthday."

They stood watching the ship get smaller and smaller until it finally disappeared, and then went back into the lounge.

Fiona took off the kimono, yawned and stretched her arms above her head. Neil could see her uptilted breasts clearly through her negligee and his heart rate quickened. He had seen her naked body more times than he could count in the time they had been together, and it never failed to arouse him.

Tonight, was no different and he nodded towards the bedroom, at the same time raising and lowering his eyebrows rapidly.

"I don't know if I like the look in your eyes, you beast. This place is obviously having an effect on you. Maybe you should sleep on the settee tonight."

Neil scooped her up in his arms, carried her through into the bedroom and dropped her onto the bed.

"No way! You've heard of the expression Droit de Seignior well tonight, *this* Seignior is having his *Droit*."

Their love making that night was not the fiery and passionate kind but more a demonstration of true love, gentle and caring. Until finally in the small hours of the morning they fell asleep in each other's arms utterly exhausted, lulled into oblivion by the smell of tropical flowers in the garden far below wafting in through the open windows, and the soothing sound of the Indian Ocean beating against the shore.

Neil was not sure what woke him. The room was still in darkness, and Fiona was lying on her back breathing softly, dead to the world. There was a gentle breeze coming through the open window and Neil could hear the mournful hooting of an owl somewhere away in the distance.

They had decided to turn off the air conditioning at night, preferring to rather have all the windows open. Air conditioning always seemed to leave them with a dried out feeling the next morning.

He got up from the bed. Yawned and stretched at the same time and walked naked through to the lounge then out onto the balcony.

After a while he found it was a bit nippy standing out there naked and went back to the bedroom for his robe. He returned to the balcony and stood silently gazing out over the invisible ocean, the owl was no longer calling, and Neil was enjoying the pre-dawn silence.

Even as he watched the sky began to slowly lose its cloak of black. Pale yellows changed to a soft peach then orange and streaks of green shot skywards, these also changed colour, and gradually the sky became red, quickly fading to a pale blue, then before he could blink everything was all blue; with the sun just making its appearance above the horizon, a new day was about to be born.

As always in the tropics the sun seemed to rise so quickly you felt you could see it moving. He wished Fiona had been there, but had he gone to call her, he knew it would have all been over before they could even get to the bedroom window. He determined that she would be there with him to watch it the next morning.

Chapter Four

They had decided that on their first day on the island they would explore the three acres of hotel garden and lounge around on the beach, just having a lazy day; but first Neil wanted to speak to Antoine about the best places to visit, and at nine thirty after a light breakfast of cereals and fruit on the verandah overlooking the garden, he asked the maître d' hotel if it would be possible for him to have a quick word with the manager.

Five minutes later Antoine, still looking immaculate came over to their table and accepted their invitation to join them for coffee. Neil explained what he wanted, and Antoine said he had just the thing for them. He called over a waiter and spoke rapidly to him, whatever it was he had said, the waiter rushed away at almost a run.

"I have sent him to my house to ask my wife for a book. This book shall be more than good for you. It will be here tout d' suite, as my house is here in the hotel garden."

Within minutes the waiter returned with an A4 sized book which he handed to Antoine; he thanked him and passed it over to Fiona. The book was written in French, but as Fiona both read and spoke the language perfectly it was not a problem.

Neil watched as she skimmed through the book. After a couple of minutes, she looked up and told him it contained more than enough information, covering everything anyone could wish to know about the history of the Seychelles, their flora and fauna and listing many places likely to be of interest to an enthusiastic tourist, with many pages of coloured photos to facilitate identification of the countless plants and birds it mentioned.

Antoine was delighted on hearing that and insisted that they accept it as a gift, but when Fiona tried to say there was no way they could accept such a valuable book, as it was a first copy signed by the author, Antoine would not take no for an answer.

"*Pas de probleme*, I have two more at my home also with the signing the professor was a good friend of my father."

Antoine explained that the book had been written by a professor Lamour who had taught biology at the island Lycée and had lived here all his life.

The professor and Antoine's father Jacques had walked many miles together around the island over several years, drawing maps and cataloguing the plant and bird life, which had resulted in the publication of the book.

Neil and Fiona were extremely touched by the gift and thanked him; he brushed their thanks to one side, and with a typical Gallic shrug of his shoulders merely said.

"It is nothing mes amies, good things are for good people."

Something that both Neil and Fiona were keen to see were the world-famous Coco de Mer palms, and when they told Antoine of their interest, he clapped his hands together.

"Bon. Tomorrow is my day off; I will ask my wife to make for us a picque-nicque and I shall take you to see the Coco de Mer. Unfortunately, we do not have them on Mahe, they grow only on the island of Pralin, but it is no problem. We can make a small flight on the aeroplane and in the Vallee de Mai, we will find them.

Neil and Fiona were delighted, and when Antoine said he would like to include his wife and their three children, as they were now on their school holidays, Neil said they would be most welcome.

Their conversation was interrupted when a porter came over and said the manager was required at the front desk; Antoine excused himself, saying.

"We can meet later for the more details. Non?"

"Fiona tapped Neil's shoulder.

27

"I'm going out to the garden…see you there."

Before joining her, Neil phoned a car hire company and arranged for a seven-seater vehicle to be at the hotel at ten the next morning, and then the airport in Victoria to hire a small plane for the crossing to the island. This done he hurried out to catch up with Fiona who was sniffing the first flowers she had come to, which just happened to be Hawaiian Ginger.

The gardens were an absolute rainbow of colours all with different scents; many of them Fiona recognised as those she had in her own garden in Muthaiga, but there were a few that neither of them had ever seen. One in particular, a really exotic plant which with the aid of the Professor's book she was able to identify as *Heliconia Robusta*, or Lobster Claw, which it did indeed resemble. There were also four more different kinds of ginger, all heavily perfumed, and all in the book.

They spent a very relaxing hour wandering through the gardens, enjoying each other's company, seeing how many different species they could find and identify, then went down to the beach.

They later found out that Antoine's father Jacques, had also designed the garden layout, and he and his friend the Professor had collected and planted all the flowers and bushes in it.

When they eventually reached the beach, Fiona ran down to the water's edge and lifting her skirts waded out to just below knee level.

"Oooh *Neil*, it is *sooo* warm, come and have a paddle."

"I can't." Neil shouted, waving the book above his head. "I'm not going to leave this on the beach. Why don't we go up and get our swimming costumes? We can have a swim, then have lunch, and make a day of it. What do you think?"

In no time at all they were back on the beach, with Fiona in a fairly modest bikini. She had wanted to wear the tanga she had bought just before leaving Nairobi. But when Neil came out of the bedroom and saw her standing in the lounge with it on, his eyes nearly popped out of his head.

"You're not going to wear *that*…*here* are you? He stammered.

"Where else, and why not my darling…don't you like it?" she teased, slowly pirouetting in front of him.

28

"Yes of course I do, but down on the beach…with all those men ogling you! I know what they will be thinking, and it's just not on. My wife in…*that*."

"Oh don't be such an old stick in the mud Neil, they won't be looking at me, they will have their girlfriends or wives with them."

But Neil thought different; Fiona could see that he was not comfortable with her in the tanga and relented.

"Okay darling, just for you I'll change," and went through into the bedroom.

Neil breathed a sigh of relief when she re-emerged wearing the bikini. They put on the hotel's light cotton robes and beach slippers and returned to the beach.

The water *was* really warm and while they frolicked happily in the light surf, they were being observed by several older couples relaxing under the palm leaf shelters on the beach, some of them with wistful looks on their faces as they remembered the time when they were that young, and love was their inspiration for life. It was obvious to the watchers that the young couple were very much in love, by the way they clung to each other and every so often kissed, blissfully unaware of the approving but also envious looks they were getting.

Lunch was a light snack of a crayfish tail salad with a bottle of nicely chilled Chenin Blanc, when that was over they went back to their apartment and spent the afternoon making love on their enormous bed, followed by a snooze which lasted until eight.

After dinner Fiona went up to the apartment saying that she was absolutely bushed.

"Go and check with Antoine that the trip to Praslin was still on," she said, "I am going to have a snooze."

Antoine said all was arranged, and suggested they had a drink at the bar. After a couple of brandies Neil went up to the apartment. Fiona fast asleep; he stood there just watching her and felt his eyes moisten, she looked so innocent and vulnerable. God how he loved this woman.

Despite Neil's resolution to wake Fiona up so they could watch the sunrise together, he slept right through until eight. He slid

29

quietly out of bed so as to not to disturb her, put on his robe and decided to do a bit of swotting up about the Coco de Mer palms.

He went through into the lounge, made himself a cup of coffee, picked up the book carried them both out onto the balcony and settled himself down on a sunbed.

"*Damn*," he said as he opened the book, he had forgotten it was in French. Still, he could at least look at the pictures.

Fiona joined him a little later, and after dressing decided they would skip breakfast, instead they just sat on the balcony drinking cups of Blue Mountain coffee and chatting about nothing in particular until a quarter to ten.

Antoine and his family were waiting for them in the lounge, and he made the introductions. His wife Lysianne was a petite dark-haired woman of about the same age as her husband. Neil noticed that she had a cheeky smile and twinkling eyes. They had three children, Marie the eldest at fifteen, Jacques thirteen and Chantal a baby girl of three, who Antoine said with a laugh was unplanned.

Fiona thought Chantal was adorable and laughed with delight when she heard the little girl try to say Fiona; the best she could manage was Fee Fee; a name that was going to stick.

Antoine suggested it would perhaps be better if he drove, and Neil was more than happy to let him. This left him free to listen as Fiona translated about the palms. He was astonished she read out that the Coco de Mer produced the largest nut in the world, which took six or seven years to mature and could weigh up to thirty kilos. There were male and female palms; the female, which could reach a height of twenty-four metres produced the nut, the male could be as high as thirty metres. Their life span was between two and four hundred years.

It took them only about forty minutes to reach the airport, and after making enquiries they were directed over to the area reserved for charter flights, where Neil remarked to Antoine about the number of charter companies offering flights to Praslin.

"This is because all the tourists want to see the Coco de Mer."

It was only a short hop to the island which lay to the northeast of Mahe, and they were hardly up before they were down.

Antoine quickly commandeered one of the many taxis waiting at the airstrip for the island's visitors and then they were on their way, he explained that he had retained the driver for the rest of the day.

Vallee de Mei was in a National Park, the name of which Neil could not pronounce, and the driver took them right up to the picnic area. There was a mad scramble from the car as all the females made a rush for the toilets, which left Neil and Antoine to unload and carry the hamper.

It seemed it was not only Neil and Fiona that had missed breakfast, so they decided to have an early lunch. Lysianne had personally prepared all the food in the hotel kitchen, and it was a meal fit for a king. The picnic was a happy occasion and the children had immaculate manners; little Chantal did manage to knock a few things over, but it was an enjoyable meal.

There was no need to go looking for the palms as they were all around them, and one palm towered above the others.

"This is the tallest tree on the island," Antoine told them proudly. "It is thirty-two metres tall."

"That is some tree," Neil said. "You know Antoine, if I hadn't seen these with my own eyes, I wouldn't believe anyone telling me how big they are."

They moved further along, and Fiona stopped directly under one palm looking upwards for a closer look at the nuts. Antoine caught hold of her shirt and pulled her back.

"Do not stand so close Fee Fee, there is too much peril." He went on to explain that a German tourist had been killed here the previous year. The unfortunate man had been kneeling to tie up a shoelace, when the palm above him decided to give birth.

Neil looked up at the truly enormous nuts, imagining one falling.

"That would definitely not be beneficial to your health," he said to Fiona.

"Maybe you have now seen enough of the Coco de Mer?" Antoine said, and suggested they take a walk through the forest. "Perhaps we can have the good luck and see our famous black parrot which live nowhere else in the world, only here in the Seychelles."

Luck did smile on them that day, because within half an hour they had seen two small flocks of parrots, about fifteen in all; Neil

31

thought them rather dowdy looking and was not impressed but did not say so.

After another hour with Chantal beginning to wilt, Lysianne thought it was time to make their way home.

When it came time to pay off their driver at the airstrip, Neil had the devil's own job to prevent Antoine from trying to pay the taxi driver.

"This trip was my idea," he insisted, "And I am going to pay, so please put your money away."

The next day, Neil and Antoine were enjoying a drink together in the lounge when Neil asked how long Antoine and his family had lived in Mahe?

"Maybe you should call Fee Fee, I think what I have to say would be of interest to her."

Neil phoned their suite and asked Fiona to come down to the lounge, as Antoine wanted to explain his family history and that of the hotel. Ten minutes later she joined them.

"My great grandfather came her with his wife and three sons many years ago but I can't remember how many. In Brittany he was the builder of boats, and here there are still boats built by them. But my father he did not want to only build boats; he wanted to be a landowner and have the hotel, et voila...the Coco de Mer."

Antoinette, Jacques wife gave birth to three sons, Antoine, Paul and Henri. He told them that he and his brothers were put into a Catholic Mission school where the Fathers were vey strict and the pupils were beaten with a bamboo cane if they were not diligent with their lessons.

"I was beaten many times, but they taught me to speak the good English. No?"

"You know Antoine, before coming here I assumed that all the hotels would be whitewashed bungalows with thatched roofs, just like you see in films about people living on a desert island."

Antoine laughed and went on to explain the development of the island's hotels.

"They were at one time, and they were very romantic and beautiful...but when the world discovered the Seychelles, alas the old-style hotels were too small." He shrugged his shoulders. "Progress monsieur, this always destroys beauty."

In the early fifties, Antoine's father decided the time had come to fulfil his dream, and together with his brothers, and aided by a loan from the Banque de Seychelles they had built Coco de Mer. Ten bungalows constructed in hand cut snow white coral blocks all thatched with coconut palm fronds.

Jacques' brothers did not want to be involved with the actual running of the hotel, and it was decided that he should manage it, while they continued with their boat building and commercial fishing.

Their venture had proved to be a great success for many years. But unfortunately, their dream began to fade as the ever-increasing number of tourists, especially the Americans, chose the more modern hotels structures with all their glass and chrome; they were more comfortable, and with their guest numbers dropping, Coc de Mer began to struggle to repay the loan.

Then came the fateful day when they were informed by the bank that if they wished to compete with the overseas property giants that were beginning to exploit the magic of the Seychelles they would have to expand. They also said they would be more than happy to extend their credit for a new hotel.

With a heavy heart and much tearful deliberation with the families, Jacques as the elder brother finally agreed that the bank experts were correct and decided that the bank were right.

He could not bring himself to stay and watch his lifelong dream being destroyed so with his wife, he went to stay with friends on the other side of the island; returning after four days to find his paradise just a patch of scarred bare earth.

On that day Antoine was already there. His parents got out of their car, and he could see them holding hands silently staring over at what had once been their whole life.

He watched them for a few minutes wanting to go over and offer some words of comfort but resisted, knowing that nothing he could say could possibly heal the hurt he knew was in the old man's heart.

One year later just a month before the new Coc de Mer was due to be completed Jacques Laporte at the age of seventy-six passed away; of a broken heart was Antoine's verdict.

33

Jacques's death was followed three months later by that of Antoinette, who had obviously decided that after fifty-seven years of never being apart from the only man she had ever loved, life without her beloved Jacques would be unacceptable; early one Sunday morning she passed quietly in her sleep. Antoine wiped a tear from his cheek and continued.

"It was fortunate for us all that while the new hotel was being built, I was sent to South Africa for the hotel management training and now here I am."

After exchanging kisses and handshakes all round, Neil and Fiona said goodnight to their host and went back to their apartment.

They had only been in the room ten minutes when the phone rang, Neil picked it up, it was Antoine.

"You have the good luck Neil. The boat company has just called to say there has been a cancellation for tomorrow, perhaps you would like to take it. No?"

Deep sea fishing was something Fiona had suggested to Neil when they had first arrived in Mahe, saying that being in the islands would be the opportunity for him to fulfil one of his life's ambitions: which was to fish for black Marlin.

Neil told her what Antoine had said.

"The weather is perfect at the moment," she said, "but it could change so why don't you go for it just in case it does."

Neil put the phone down and gave her a hug.

"Great, but you are coming with me…no arguments." She nodded, and Neil picked up the phone.

"Would you call them back please Antoine and confirm the booking?"

Chapter Five

Neil had requested a four thirty wake up call, and was surprised when instead of the phone ringing, there was a knock at the door. Neil slipped on his dressing gown and went to see who it was. He opened it, and there was Antoine, with a tray of steaming coffee for them; he said he would see them in the foyer at five, and on arrival they found him waiting for them with a large wicker hamper ready to be put into the boot of their car.

In the time they had been there, Antoine had become more than just the manager, he was now a friend, and although Neil was in no doubt that Fiona was probably the main attraction, the man obviously liked Neil very much.

The cross-country drive in their rented BMW took them just over three quarters of an hour. And Antoine had been right, apart from two or three lorries and a couple of horse drawn carts, theirs was the only vehicle on the road.

Just as dawn was breaking, they pulled into the Marina car park, where they saw three men standing at the edge of the jetty. Neil parked under a huge mango tree, and they got out of the car. He unloaded the hamper from the boot, and then locked up. By this time, the men had reached the car, and Neil turned to speak to them. One of the men spoke.

"Monsieur Owens?" he asked.

"Yes," Neil replied.

"Good morning Monsieur, Madame. My name is Guy Sauvage."

He shook Neil's hand and kissed Fiona on both cheeks.

"These men are my crew, Renan and Pierre. They all shook hands, and at the skipper's suggestion made their way over to his boat, with the two crewmen carrying the hamper.

"Have you noticed Neil, all the kissing that goes on here?" Fiona whispered.

"That's the French for you."

The charter boat was a very trim professional looking craft. At thirty-five feet long, with its immaculate white and pale blue paint gleaming in the early morning sunlight, it was obviously much loved and well cared for.

Neil noticed with amusement that the boat's name was *Erotique*, he nudged Fiona to attract her attention, and nodded at the name, she smiled and nudged him back. Neil was tempted to ask Guy the origin of the name but decided against it.

They went on board. Guy fired the engine, and ten minutes later, with Neil and Fiona enjoying the view from reclining chairs on the flying bridge, cups of rich dark coffee supplied by Renan in their hands, they were well on their way to the area Guy had decided on for that day.

As they were clearing the headland to the south of the marina, Neil asked Guy how the place had got its name?

"If you look to your left side Monsieur, you will see why…you understand that Nez Noir means black nose."

Neil looked over. They were passing very close to a section of black rock jutting out into the water, and the outline was very much like a human head with a prominent nose. 'Well named,' he thought.

By seven they were about twenty miles out from Nez Noir. Neil, sitting in the fighting chair at the stern was beginning to feel a little disheartened. For over an hour Guy had piloted the boat back and forward over his chosen fishing ground, but so far there had not been a single strike. Every so often when Neil looked up at him on the flying bridge, Guy would make signs with his hands that clearly meant patience my friend, patience. By nine he was considering saying maybe they should go back, but he remembered Antoine's words about the skipper's reputation.

Meanwhile, with the sun climbing majestically into a cloudless sky, Fiona, liberally coated with sunscreen was happily sunbathing on the cabin roof. And undressed as she was, in her bikini, she had, with no effort at all, succeeded in making Renan and Pierre the two happiest crewmen in the Seychelles.

Neil looked up but couldn't see her. But Renan and Pierre were now cleaning the bridge fittings for the umpteenth time since she had gone up there. Neil was surprised at Guy being so free and easy with them. There again, there wasn't much else for them to do, and a beautiful woman on the boat now and then must be one of the perks of the job.

Neil took a quick look at his watch…nine thirty. Much to the crewmen's dismay Fiona had folded her towel and gone down to the salon to read. He looked back across the water to where he could just make out his line hissing through the wave tops.

At that same moment, the line snapped free of the outrigger above him, and the sudden massive jerk nearly took his arms from their sockets. At Guy's shout, Pierre rushed astern and fastened the clamps on Neil's body harness onto the fighting chair.

Neil had seen films of fisherman trying to land a marlin and had read many books about it, but nothing had prepared him for what he was now experiencing. If it wasn't for the fact that he was strapped in, he would probably be far behind the boat now, water skiing his way to Australia.

His line was running out so fast that the massive reel was beginning to smoke. Pierre poured a bucket of water on it, and the steam rose into Neil's face making his eyes water. He looked down at the reel in dismay. It was more than half empty, if his fish did not turn soon, he was going to be out of line.

Guy was helping him by piloting the boat in reverse, to try and ease the strain on the line, which suddenly went slack, then began making its way towards him.

Guy slammed the engine into forward and shouted for Neil to 'reel in like hell!' This whole procedure repeated itself time and again for two hours, until Neil felt he was going to die of exhaustion. Sweat streamed from every pore in his body; his hands were blistered, and he knew that his bum was, even though the seat was padded.

Standing alongside him, with the bucket of water ready to cool down the reel, Pierre had indicated several times that Neil was into a really big fish; but this was information that Neil was more than aware of.

After what seemed an eternity, the equally exhausted fish came alongside. Pierre unclipped Neil from the chair, and Neil gratefully handed him the rod; while Renan got ready to gaff the marlin. As he leant over the side, Fiona screamed and grabbed hold of Renan's arm.

"*No* Neil, *please…* let it go."

Neil leant over the side and looked down at the animal that had fought him valiantly for so many hours. The marlin was at least eight feet long and its black shiny skin was a myriad of thousands of all colours of the rainbow as it twisted and turned in the side wash from the now almost stationary boat. Its uppermost eye looked up at Neil, and he felt a lump rise in his throat as he saw the defiance still shining fiercely there.

He so much wanted to take his trophy back to Nez Noir, and have his photograph taken with it. Something to show off to his friends; then in his mind's eye he saw the pictures of other marlin suspended by their tails from the gantry, stripped of dignity and the vibrant colours of life, surrounded by men grinning like idiots…Fiona was right!

He nodded at Guy who was standing at his side, with Pierre now at the wheel. Guy leant down to the water and quickly cut through the shank of the hook with a pair of long handled bolt cutters.

For a split second the marlin stayed there looking up at him, and Neil felt certain the look in its eye had turned from defiance to gratitude. Then with one mighty flick of its crescent tail it was gone, back to its kingdom in the depths of the Indian Ocean.

Neil felt someone pulling at his arm and turned. It was Fiona, tears were streaming down her face as she said.

"That was the most noble thing I think any man could ever do; I know how much you wanted to keep him…I'm so proud of you my darling."

Guy reached across and put his arm across Neil's shoulders.

"Bravo mon ami."

Guy had taken many men out to hunt for the much sought after and extremely elusive black marlin; his clients had caught many while in his expert hands, but this was the sort of man he preferred, a *real* sportsman.

They opened and drank the bottle of champagne Antoine had included in the hamper. He had carefully wrapped it in insulating foil, and it was still acceptably cold. In all the excitement, none of

39

them had remembered the food, and rather than offend Antoine by taking it back, Neil invited Guy and his men to share it with them.

After docking back at Nez Noir, Neil shook Guy's hand.

"I cannot thank you enough, this has been a day I will remember for the rest of my life.

Guy looked into Neil's eyes.

"The pleasure was mine. She was beautiful, no?"

A slightly puzzled Neil stammered.

"She…?"

"The fish Monsieur…the fish…was she not beautiful?"

Neil agreed with him and this gave him an opening to enquire about the boat's name.

"If you don't mind me asking Guy, why did you call your boat *Erotique*?'"

"I don't mind at all Monsieur," he answered with an enigmatic smile, "she is named after my wife."

On their way to Nez Noir, they had passed several roadside market stalls being set up, for the start of the new day. Secretly Neil had hoped that Fiona had not noticed them as the stall holders worked away by the light of pressure lamps, ready for the hoped-for hundreds of 'spend happy' tourists that flocked to these markets like moths to a flame. But she *had* noticed and asked if they could stop for a quick look on their way back? He sighed, knowing full well what Fiona's quick look meant, but said that would be fine.

This must have been a special market for some reason or other, and although the stalls were all very much alike, the people running them, and the things they were selling were a world apart; even Neil, a typical man as regards shopping, had to agree with her that this market was something special.

Markets were always busy, but this one was way over the top. There were so many people pushing and shoving each other round the stalls that you virtually had to keep your arms down by your side. As for walking together, that was totally out of the question, you just had to make your way as best as you could, at the same time trying to keep each other in sight.

The aroma coming from the food being cooked over the numerous charcoal fires smelt so appetizing, that despite having eaten on the boat, they thought they might just have a snack.

The food appeared to be of a very high standard, and neither of them could recall ever seeing so many different choices of meat, but dining there that day, was out of the question; there were dozens of people around the fires, all wanting to eat at the same time.

Finally even Fiona had had enough, which surprised Neil, as an ardent shopper she never gave in, but the size of this crowd had overwhelmed even her, but it was not until they got back to the BMW that Neil realised just how much noise the market had been; it was one continuous roar.

They reached their car at the same time as a young couple, obviously Seychellois, parked, alongside, and Neil asked why there were so many people around. The man told him that today was a big annual event, with healers and their medicines visiting from all around the islands.

They set off, and a little further up the road spotted a small bistro called La Jaune Grenouille; The Yellow Frog. Fiona liked the name so much she asked Neil to stop, and they had a surprisingly good light lunch, a sort of vegetable curry, washed down with fresh coconut milk, straight out of the green coconut.

As they pulled up at the front of the hotel, Neil couldn't help wondering why the valet, waiting to park the BMW had an ear-splitting grin on his face. Fiona and Neil looked at each other and Neil shrugged his shoulders, 'just *what* did the man know that they didn't?' They were about to find out.

Guy must have phoned Antoine and given him a blow for blow account of the morning's trip. Antoine looked as proud as if his wife had just given birth to triplets, and he rushed forward to greet them.

"Oh, Neil, Feefee, Guy has told me that you are catching the biggest fish he has seen for long years. What a pity you don't bring him to the hotel. What dinners we could make for you."

Neil could just imagine what the car hire people would have thought, if they had seen one of their, top of the range beamers, with two feet of smelly fish sticking out either side of the back windows.

"Never mind Neil, I do understand. You catch the beautiful fish and then let him go; this is the English sporting...*Non*? Come, we have champagne for you and Madame Feefee in the lounge."

41

By the time they reached the lounge, Neil's back was quite sore from all the people slapping him on the back and congratulating him, staff, and guests alike.

"It was only a damn fish," he complained to Fiona, "and don't they have anything to drink except champagne?"

She could see that secretly; Neil was lapping up all the attention. It was probably more than he would have got if they had brought it back with them.

Later that night after a particularly brilliant marathon bedroom performance by Neil, Fiona lay back literally purring with contentment and thinking. 'I must take him fishing more often', then she rolled over and snuggled up against him.

"Neeeil.....pleeese" she breathed into his ear.

He turned towards her and opened one eye.

"I couldn't my darling, not again, not even if you begged me."

"Fat chance of me doing that you bighead, and anyway that isn't what I want; what do you think I am, a nymphomaniac?"

Neil smiled, thinking, 'I wish.'

"Do you think we could do bit of market shopping tomorrow?"

"For you, my darling...anything, now can I please get some sleep?"

Neil woke with a start, and noted it was still dark. He looked at the bedside clock, which showed 0515. He groaned and sat up. In his dreams he had been back in the fighting chair, battling to reel in the black marlin; the same fish, but this time he was going to bring it on board. He manoeuvred it alongside, and just as Renan was about to gaff it, he woke up.

He went through into the lounge and prepared a pot of coffee. When it was ready, he put it on a tray with two cups, and milk and sugar and took it through to the bedroom.

Fiona was still sound asleep lying on her back with her mouth slightly open. He put the tray on the bedside table and shook her gently, her eyes half opened, and she murmured.

"I couldn't my darling, not again, not even if you begged me."

She then snatched up a pillow and hit him over the head with it. "I vaguely heard you get up," she said, laughing at him as he tried to spit a feather out of his mouth. "Then I smelt that lovely coffee, and I was awake; come back to bed!"

"No way, you are going to watch the sun come up with me." He pulled the duvet off her and dragged her halfway down the bed.

"*Alright. Alright.* I give in. I'll be with you in two ticks, I just need to go to the loo."

Neil went out onto the balcony, the sky was no longer deep black, and he knew the miracle was about to begin, and shouted to her.

"Come on Fiona, you're going to miss it." He heard the toilet flush, and then she was next to him.

Dawn that morning was a replica of the first one Neil had seen, only more so. For some reason, the colours seemed even more intense. Fiona gripped his arm.

"Have you *ever* seen anything so beautiful?"

"I knew you would like it darling, that's why I got you up."

They stood watching until the full sun was showing and then went back to bed. They didn't plan to leave until after breakfast, so there was plenty of time for a snooze...or whatever.

Chapter Six

They must have visited at least five markets that day; Neil stopped keeping score at three, and it took up the whole day. Although like most men Neil hated shopping, he had to admit these markets really were something else. Antoine had told them the islands had two official languages; French and English, but Creole seemed to be the most widely used, around the markets.

They could not believe the range of things on sale. Fruit and vegetables, some of which they had never seen before, let alone heard of. Exotic spices and perfumes, native jewellery, hats, scarves, and skirts in mind blowing colours.

There were birds in bamboo cages, walking sticks and wicked looking knives in sharkskin sheaths alongside stalls selling the latest thing in 35mm cameras. And every stall seemed to have something different to offer that the others had not.

Neither of them had realised that people were made in so many varieties of colour, nor so many different facial types. The markets really were human melting pots.

About every fourth stall seemed to be cooking and selling food, with dozens of menus to choose from, and seemingly no two stalls offering the same thing.

Around mid-day, at one not so busy market Fiona suggested they get something to eat. She picked a stall she liked the look of, they made their purchase, and walked along chomping away at a mixture of prawns and fish wrapped in some sort of chapatti. It was delicious, and they thought they would like some more. But this was not to be, they couldn't find the same stall again.

45

They stopped at another market, where Fiona purchased a hand embroidered Japanese Kimono for her mother, and an exquisitely carved ashtray made of deep green jade for her father, while Neil bought a double row of freshwater pearls for Jean, his long-suffering secretary.

It was almost dark by the time they reached the hotel, where they found a very anxious Antoine pacing up and down the foyer, waiting to invite them for dinner. He rushed over and shook Neil's hand, then kissed Fiona on both cheeks.

"I was beginning to be worried that perhaps you have had an accident. My Lysianne has made for you a special dinner tonight at my house, and we would very much love you to come…Oui?"

Fiona was delighted at the invitation and asked if Chantal would still be awake when they arrived?

"But of course, my dear, all day she has speak of nothing but, when will her Aunty Feefee be here? Seven o' clock is good for you perhaps?"

It turned out to be a wonderful evening; the main dish was an arrangement of several different sorts of fish, which Lysianne had marinated in a coconut and curry sauce, served on a bed of brown rice mixed with tiny pieces of sweet potato and garlic. For dessert she had prepared a fruit cocktail that contained pieces of fruit of every variety available on the island.

A highly delighted Chantal had spent most of the evening on Fiona's lap, and was over the moon when Fiona asked Lysianne if she could put the little girl to bed. When she came back, both Neil and Antoine noticed that she had a strange sort of dreamy look. Antoine looked over at Neil and shrugged his shoulders, while his wife, recognising that look for what it was, smiled at the expression on Neil's face.

One evening Neil was having a drink at the hotel bar with Antoine, when he mentioned what a pity it was that the Coco de Mer was no longer as it had been when Jacque had first started in the hotel business.

Antoine, who just about to take a swallow of his drink paused, looked at Neil and asked him why?

"Well, it's just that the picture we had in our minds, is that there were places to stay like this hotel was, when your father first built it. Fiona was hoping to spend a couple of nights in one of them…you know the sort of romantic ideas women get.'

Antoine slapped Neil on the back and laughed.

"Your problem she is no more mon ami. I have such a place, and it can be at your use anytime."

"That would be fantastic…are you sure Antoine?"

Antoine explained that his father had owned a three-acre plot of beachfront, one kilometre south of a small town called Belle Ombre on Northwest Bay. After his death, his sons had inherited it, and they had divided it into three; one plot each.

There had been no buildings there, so Antoine and his brothers had each built a small house, which they were able to connect up to the town's water and electricity.

"My papa called his cottage Quelle Fleur, because when Marie was small, and he take her in the garden, she always say, what is this flower grandpere, what is this flower?" He laughed at the memory.

"'My brothers live there all the time, and we go for the holidays and some weekends, it is a most beautiful place, your Feefee will be so happy."

As soon as Neil went back to their apartment, he called out.

"Tomorrow night my darling, and the night after, we will be sleeping, in someone else's beds, but it is a secret …so you will have to wait to find out where."

Fiona rushed across and took his face in both hands.

"If you think I am going to be satisfied with only that much information, you have another think coming my boy, so think again."

But no matter what she tried; she could not get anything else from him. He just kept telling her she would have to wait until tomorrow night.

It was not until later when they were in bed, and she had begun kissing his neck and nibbling his ears that he finally capitulated and told her they were going to be spending two nights at a beach cottage called Quelle Fleur on Northwest Bay. Neil knew that she was going to be pleased, but when she started jumping up and down on the bed, clapping her hands, and shouting.

47

"*Yes…Yes…Yes,*" at the top of her voice, he guessed she was more than pleased.

He pulled her down onto the bed.

"For God's sake Fiona," he hissed in her ear, "have you forgotten there are people on the other side of that wall, what the hell do you think they will think is going on in here?"

The next morning just after breakfast and following the map and directions Antoine had given them, they set out for Quelle Fleur. Antoine had especially chosen the long way round, which would give them a chance see a bit more of the island before returning home.

Neil drove at a leisurely rate north along the coast road with its wonderful views of the ocean. Antoine had told them it was about twenty-five miles, so allowing for stops along the way to sightsee, Neil estimated they should be there by ten…ten thirty.

They stopped briefly at Anse Royale to fill up with petrol, and as they drove on after passing the Airport on their left, then the small town of Cascade, they could clearly see Cerf Island across the Cerf Passage. It was a beautiful day, as it had been for the whole of their visit, and the weather forecast was good for many days to come.

Fiona suggested they stop for groceries at a supermarket in Victoria.

"We didn't ask Antoine about buying food when we get there," she said, "but he did say not to buy any fish. The local fishermen land their catch every evening, at about five, on the beach below the cottage…maybe we could have fish tonight, he said there was a barbecue grill in the garden."

The previous day Neil had gone into town and changed their hatchback for a convertible, now cruising along with the top down; mountains on their left and brilliant blue water to their right it was a breath-taking drive.

Eventually the road began to turn towards the east as they reached the northern most part of Mahé, then after about a mile and a half, it ran due south, and in no time at all they were passing through Belle Ombre.

Fiona as navigator consulted Antoine's directions.

"He says it is about three miles the other side of whatever that place was called, and we have to watch out for a white board nailed to a coconut tree, with Quelle Fleur on it."

The words were hardly out of her mouth when Neil spotted the sign and swung right down a sandy road towards the beach.

He parked the car in front of what Antoine had described as a cottage, which was in reality, the understatement of the year. Built from white coral blocks, the roof was thatched with coconut palm leaves, and there was a wide verandah, which ran around all four sides of the house, with comfortable looking chairs and small tables everywhere; the wooden uprights supporting the verandah roof each had a different colour bougainvillea growing up it. The whole setting was magnificent. Fiona stood with one hand up to her mouth.

"Oh Neil this is *so* beautiful…when I see something like this, it makes me wish I could paint…I could stay here for ever."

"Well unfortunately we only have two days, so let's make the best of it. What did Antoine say about the house keys?"

"He said they were with his brothers."

"Yes darling, but which one?"

"They *both* have keys Neil, one lives that way, and the other lives that way," she said pointing left and right..."take your pick."

Neil chose the one to the right and they set off through the garden. You could tell that it had been laid out by the same person who had created the gardens at the hotel; someone who knew his flowers and loved gardens. It was an absolute riot of colour, added to by dozens of brightly painted butterflies flitting from flower to flower.

There were no fences dividing the three properties and it was impossible to know when you went from one brother's garden to the next, as Jacques Laporte had planted all three of them.

They heard a dog bark, and a small ball of hair on long thin legs rushed out from behind an oleander bush, it began jumping up and down and barking. It was soon joined by a man that could easily have been Antoine's twin; this *had* to be one of his brothers.

He extended his hand.

"Bonjour Monsieur...Madame, you are the friends of mon frere Antoine...No? My name is Paul, welcome to Quelle Fleur." The dog was still jumping up and down like a hairy tennis ball on steroids.

"Feefee...*shut up*," he roared, and it did. He didn't see the smiles on Neil and Fiona's faces, when they heard the dog's name. 'That was something Antoine forgot to tell us,' Neil thought.

Paul must have heard them drive up, as he already had the keys in his hand. He walked them back to Quelle Fleur, with a now silent Feefee trotting along ahead. On reaching the cottage he handed them the keys, and after wishing them a happy stay, said 'au revoir' and went back through the garden.

Neil heard a whining noise and looked down, Feefee was gazing up at him, with an expression that clearly said, 'I can stay if you have biscuits,' but then a piercing whistle from its master had it running off at top speed, barking its head off.

"You had a new friend there for a little while Neil." Fiona said with a laugh, "and his master didn't stay around for long either did he?"

What neither of them knew, was that when Antoine had phoned his brothers to say they were coming, he had said to leave them alone, they were on their honeymoon; but to keep an eye open to make sure they had no problems.

Fiona looked at her watch.

"It's almost eleven, do you feel like a walk along the beach to see if there is somewhere nice to have lunch?"

"Good idea girl, but we'd better take our bags in first...we can unpack when we come back."

The cottage had no ceiling, and the roof was supported by massive rafters of some dark wood.

"No need for air conditioning here," Neil remarked, "I like it."

There were two bedrooms, one, obviously the master bedroom with an en suite bathroom, a nice sized lounge, and a kitchen that had Fiona rubbing her hands with glee.

Neil noticed this and laughed.

"Don't get too excited darling, you won't be spending much time in there."

Fiona put her hands up in front of her face, palms outwards in mock horror.

50

"I'm sure I don't know what you mean sir."

"What I mean is…that we are going down the beach for lunch now, tonight we're having a barbie, and tomorrow we will probably do the same. I don't want you in the kitchen when we could be out on the beach, in fact I don't know why we brought food with us at all…except for breakfast, that's what I meant you hussy."

They had a quick wash and set off down through the front garden to the beach. Apart from all the flowers and flowering shrubs, there were coconut palms, wild almond and cashew nut trees, frangipani, and casuarinas everywhere.

"I really would like to have met Antoine's father," Fiona said wistfully. "Anybody that has such an eye for beauty must be a really good person."

Neil stepped back and pinched her bottom playfully.

"That must include me as well then my little watermelon…because I certainly had an eye for you." He ran past and waited for her on the beach.

They stood together looking up and down the beach; there was not a soul in sight.

"Which way then girl?" Neil asked.

Fiona looked left and right, and then chose right. They had only walked about three hundred yards when they heard music. There was a footpath leading away from the beach, they turned onto it and had to walk single file. It wound its way through a coconut palm plantation for about fifty yards, until there in front of them was a small restaurant. The music was coming from an old wind-up gramophone on a table on the front verandah, and five or six people were sitting around it with drinks in their hands.

A small man with a white apron jumped up and stepped off the verandah to greet them. Neil and Fiona looked at each other in surprise when the man said.

"Bonjour Monsieur Owens…Madame…welcome."

Neil looked at Fiona and shrugged. Was there anyone up here that Antoine had not told they were coming?

The man told them he was the owner and knew the Laporte families well. He cooked them an excellent meal of chicken and spiced rice with sweet potatoes, which they washed down with a few glasses of cold white wine. He asked them questions about

51

themselves, where they came from and what they did. Then he told them some of the history of that part of Mahé, he really was a fount of knowledge, and it was just after two when he finally let them leave.

Back at Quelle Fleur they found little Feefee standing guard outside, but she ran away when they invited her in. Fiona laughed.

"She's probably gone to tell Paul we've come back."

Neil suggested a little siesta.

"Then we can go down on the beach when the fishermen come in at about four thirty. Antoine says they land their catch here because he lets them use his road."

Neil woke to the faint sound of someone shouting, and then several men laughing. He looked at his watch, it showed a quarter to five, 'probably the fishermen,' he thought. Fiona was still fast asleep, so he shook her shoulder until she was awake.

"Oh Neil!" she said as she yawned and stretched her arms above her head. "Did you have to do that? I was having such a lovely dream."

"Yes, I did, that's if you want fish for supper."

By the time they got down to the water, the fishermen had already boxed up their day's catch and were loading it onto a trolley. All of them were smiling when Neil called out.

"Bonjour," and he felt a little disappointed when they answered "bonjour," without the expected "Monsieur Owens.'"

Fiona with her French was able to make a deal for some nice plump red snapper, and the men were so impressed with her, they threw in a fair-sized rock cod for free.

Back at the cottage, while Neil started the coals going, Fiona made them a salad. When this was done, she helped him carry the two-seater settee off the verandah and down into the garden; she had chosen a spot right next to a night flowering jessamine, and the scent from the flowers that only opened in the evening, was almost overpowering.

Having fish fresh from the sea, was always a treat for people who lived inland in Kenya, and Neil had grilled the red snappers to perfection.

After eating, they lay back on the settee quietly sipping gin and tonics watching the sun setting; they could see the palm trees in front of them slowly changing from their natural colour, to become fluffy black topped poles against a dark blue backdrop, until finally they disappeared completely, and became part of the night.

An almost full moon began rising from the ocean, and now, still low on the horizon it was sending a stream of light across the water towards them, a magical highway of silver.

They sat out until eleven, just talking and cuddling and listening to the waves lapping against the shore before going off to bed. That night they made love until they finally fell asleep in each other's arms, exhausted and blissfully happy.

It was midday before they woke that morning, and after a very late breakfast they spent the afternoon just lazing around on the beach with an occasional swim to cool down.

That evening Fiona baked the rock cod in wine, served it with salad, and after another evening of lying back and just enjoying the tranquillity, they went to bed early to spend their last night in Quelle Fleur.

The next morning, they had another late breakfast at ten, and after clearing up the cottage, they went to return the house keys to Paul, taking with them almost all the groceries they had brought with them, which they gave to him.

Paull suggested they try a different way back, and with the help of an old map they he had, they planned their route. He said that it was a very picturesque road, but it was not possible to go any further south from Belle Ombre they would first have to drive across the island back to Victoria.

At Victoria, Neil drove southwest to Port Glaud then followed the coast road south before cutting across to Anse Royale, then finally 'home'; Paul had been right about that route being picturesque.

They were welcomed back by the Laportes like a long-lost family and spent the evening with them followed by dinner at their house, with Antoine asking several times.

"If   everything   was   good   for   you?"

Chapter Seven

The rest of the holiday just went by in a blur, with endless trips to places of interest recommended by Antoine, dining out, sometimes staying to dance, and hours of swimming and lying on the beach.

The only thing they did not do was go scuba diving. Fiona couldn't stand the thought of being underwater like that, depending on a small metal bottle for her air.

Although Neil as an experienced diver would have liked to have gone out to the island reefs, it didn't faze him all that much, as he had spent many hours under water in the Kenya coastal waters and knew the fish and corals would be very similar. He had had fantastic day black marlin fishing, and after all, it was her holiday, as well as his.

The night before they were due to fly out, they took Antoine and Lysianne out for a farewell and thank you dinner at a restaurant they had eaten at a few times; again one of Antoine's' recommendations, La Langoustine.

It had been a wonderful evening, a mixture of both joy and sorrow, joy because they had all met, and sorrow that after becoming such good friends they were having to part. Neil could not thank Antoine enough for everything he and his family had done for them both, adding that the holiday would not have been so perfect if it had not been for their kindness.

Antoine had tears in his eyes when he said how much they enjoyed having them at his hotel, and that Neil and Feefee were now part of his family. Then when Neil said they hoped Antoine and his family would not leave it too long before they came to Nairobi as the Owens' guests, Lysianne began to cry quietly, this in turn started Fiona off, and Neil, noticed they were beginning to get looks of sympathy from people at the tables around them, most likely thinking they had just experienced a family tragedy.

But the evening ended with smiles, and they drove back to the hotel happy in the knowledge that invitations to visit each other had been offered and accepted.

The next morning while Neil sat having a beer with Antoine, Fiona walked with Lysianne and Chantal around the garden. In the afternoon, after a rousing '*au revoir*' from the entire staff, several of them happily tucking lavish tips into their pockets, Antoine, accompanied by his family, drove them out to the airport, where there were more tearful goodbyes before they boarded the Air Seychelles flight taking them home.

The 737 touched down at Nairobi International just as the sun was going down behind the Ngong Hills, Neil had specifically asked for a window seat so he could see them. Whenever he returned to Nairobi by air, he knew he was really home as soon as he caught sight of the hills with their four distinctive peaks.

Duncan and a Moira bursting to know all the details of their honeymoon were waiting for them as they cleared the always tiresome customs and immigration departments.

"We have a meal waiting for you at home," Duncan told them as they got into his car. "Then I can run you back to Muthaiga."

He drove off with Neil in the front with him, and Fiona trapped in the back with her mother, who was vociferously pumping her for more and more information, saying she wanted to know *everything.*

Neil chatted away to Duncan just really making small talk to pass the time. Every now and again he could hear bits and pieces of the mainly one-sided conversation from the back, and was relieved that so far it did not contain the 'everything' parts that Moira was really interested in.

At the house, Duncan said there was no point in unloading their luggage, only to have to put it all back in again when he took them home.

Fiona noticed the look on her mother's face, knowing immediately what she was thinking, 'that means I'm not going to get my present until tomorrow.'

"Don't worry mother, I have yours and dad's presents in my carry-on bag."

They went into the lounge and while Fiona and her mother went of to the kitchen to get the dinner organised, Duncan poured Neil a single malt. Neil looked around the room, something was puzzling him, it somehow seemed different. Duncan came over with his drink.

"I know my boy, looks better now doesn't it, with all that crap out of the place."

Straight away Neil knew what it was what was. All the ghastly china dogs that had been dotted round the room were gone, now replaced by Duncan's choice, native made soapstone carvings.

Neil had once counted the dogs, there were fifteen of them, and they really were hideous. The sort of thing you would be presented with at a fairground game of skill if you were unlucky enough to win.

Moira had been collecting the dogs for a number of years, ever since the husband of one of her friends, obviously one with a sense of humour, told her the one she had, would become a collectible item.

Ever since then, she scoured the car boot sales held every Saturday at Karen and was always over the moon if she ever found one for sale, especially as she always got them for a few measly shillings.

Duncan explained the reason for their absence, and the day the bottom fell out Moira's collectors' world.

"We had a visitor over for Sunday lunch while you were away. He is a well-known authority on china and porcelain, and I had invited him over to talk about him joining the club, and you know Moira, she saw it as a chance to get a free appraisal. Unfortunately, it all backfired."

Moira was beside herself with excitement, and she had deliberately not mentioned her dogs to the guest over lunch. She wanted to see the look on his face when on entering the lounge for coffee he would discover her treasures.

He certainly noticed them alright. Moira had carefully arranged them all together in a line along the mantle piece. But even freshly dusted and shining with furniture polish they still looked hideous.

The expert had walked straight over to the mantelpiece and stood looking at them. Moira, bursting with pride could hardly contain herself as she waited for the praise she knew was forthcoming.

"Very interesting, I have never seen so many of these things in one place."

Moira took a deep breath and looked over at Duncan with a look of triumph. He had always hated the damn things *but* had put up with them because he loved her. 'Here it comes,' she thought.

"These are what my South African friend would call Afrikaans Jewish Renaissance. I presume you have them all together ready to take them to a charity shop. I'm sure you will be able to find one that will have them."

Poor old Moira had collapsed back into an armchair which luckily was right behind her. The expert looked most concerned and looked at Duncan who was now kneeling by her side.

"Sorry about that old chap," Duncan said, "she's been down with a touch of malaria recently, I did tell her she should stay in bed today."

With the bitterly disillusioned Moira tucked away in bed, weeping into her hanky, and a cold flannel on her forehead, Duncan entertained their guest for a while, until he rose, thanked him for their hospitality and left, saying, he hoped that Mrs McDonald would soon be better.

The next morning while Moira was still in her bed, Duncan put the china dogs, which he now knew Moira would never want to see again, in two cardboard boxes into the boot of his car, took them down to the city, and gave them to a charity shop.

Duncan put his hand on Neil's arm.

"For God's sake whatever you do man, do not mention them at all, will you? And tell Fiona the same."

Fiona came in to say dinner was on the table and Neil quickly whispered to her not to say anything about the china dogs. Fiona looked around the room, noticing for the first time that the dogs were indeed gone. She opened her mouth for an explanation.

"Don't ask, I'll tell you when we get home."

After dinner, with another of father in law's single malts under his belt, Neil and Fiona got into the back of the Bentley, and Duncan drove them home, leaving Moira happily parading in front of her bedroom mirror, dressed in the exquisitely embroidered Japanese kimono.

Back at Muthaiga, Duncan refused the offer of a night cap and with a sharp toot on the horn drove away. Although they both loved the old man, they were pleased that he had turned down their offer, and although their two weeks on Mahé had been something they would remember for the rest of their lives, they were glad to be home; it had been a long day, and their bed was calling them.

Chapter Eight

Neil looked at Fiona's face smiling back at him from the photo on his desk and could hardly believe it was two years since it had been taken on their honeymoon on Mahé. He had only been in his office for fifteen minutes, and this was the third or fourth time his eyes had been drawn to it, like a needle to a magnet. Fiona's smile was one of the first things that most people noticed when first meeting her. That was after they had recovered from seeing her stunning looks, next were her eyes, pools of mystery and passion where a man could easily drown, without making any effort to save himself.

Their honeymoon had been almost magical, so much in love and so happy together. They had been back to Mahé once since then and had spent a fantastic week staying with their friends.

Antoine had taken the week off, and they had hired a forty-foot yacht, spending their time leisurely cruising from island to island, and mooring up for the night wherever took their fancy. Little Chantal was Fiona's constant shadow for the whole week, and

Antoine had written and told them she had cried the whole day after they had gone.

The Antoine family were such good people, and Neil and Fiona felt privileged to have them as friends.

The Laportes had come over to Kenya the year after that, and Neil and Fiona had planned a holiday for them they would never forget.

On their second night in Kenya, Duncan and Moira had invited the Laportes over for dinner, and Antoine was very impressed when they pulled up at the McDonald's front door in Neil's Range Rover to see Duncan dressed in his full Highland dress waiting to welcome them.

The two men got on very well together, and Duncan was more than pleased to have found someone who really enjoyed a good single malt, unlike Neil, who Duncan said, 'only drank it.'

A few nights later, Moira kindly offered to baby sit for them, and Neil and Fiona were able to show Antoine and Lysianne some of Nairobi's hot spots; Lysianne particularly liked the Equator Club.

It amused Neil that wherever they ate out, Antoine was continually casting his hotelier's eye critically around.

Fiona took Lysianne shopping one day, and when they returned, Neil saw Lysianne's purchases, and was convinced that she was taking things back that she could have bought in any of the Mahé markets, and probably cheaper.

"Talk about coals to Newcastle," he had whispered in Fiona's ear. Only to receive a sharp dig in the ribs, and a glare that nearly blistered his face.

Neil wanted the Laportes' holiday, to be one they would remember for a long time. He had already contacted an old school friend, Peter Allen, who ran a safari company, 'Animals Unlimited', and had made a booking for a two-week safari.

Peter was a very experienced operator, so Neil knew he was getting the best.

Peter had drawn up an itinerary one evening over drinks at the Long Bar with Neil, which would give the Laportes a good overview of Kenya with its wide range of landscapes, and Neil knew that

Peter would definitely find all the right animals, especially the Big Five; Rhino, buffalo, lion, leopard and the biggest of the five, elephant.

Peter came up trumps with the animals, with one leopard, fifteen rhinos; one of which chased their Land Rover for a while, before giving up. Neil had laughingly said that although rhinos had very poor hearing, even this one had not been able to take the screaming coming from all the females in the vehicle. They had seen countless numbers of elephant and buffalos, and several prides of lions.

They stayed for one night at an hotel on the shore of Lake Victoria, and that evening, standing looking out across the waters of the Lake, Antoine could not quite grasp its immensity, after Neil had told him it covered an area of sixty-four thousand square miles, and after a bit of quick mental arithmetic, the realisation that his beloved Mahé, at sixty square miles, could fit into the lake just over a thousand times, absolutely astounded him.

Peter drove them through the forests of the Aberdare Mountains, with wonderful views of Mount Kenya. Then it was back to Nairobi.

After a day of relaxing around the house, Neil drove them down to the New Stanley Grill in the city for a meal. Leaving the children in the care of a babysitter Fiona had arranged for the evening.

He wanted the Laporte's last night in Nairobi to be one to remember, and when he heard that there was to be troupe of Georgian dancers performing at the Grill, he had immediately booked a table for them.

It was a fantastic evening, and watching the dancers perform, Neil remarked to Antoine that he had never seen anything like it in all his life. Antoine agreed with him and said that perhaps he ought to bring acts like this to Mahé.

"It would be very good for my business," he said with a laugh.

While they were busy talking, several of the male dancers left the group, came over to Neil's table and dragged a very embarrassed Lysianne and Fiona, and two ladies from the next table out onto the dance floor, to teach them Cossack dancing.

It was an absolute riot, and after ten minutes of being whirled round and round, Lysianne and Fiona, both red faced and out of breath had to plead exhaustion before they were allowed to go back to the table. The rest of the diners had participated whole-heartedly, clapping, and cheering, and calling out encouragement whenever either Lysianne or Fiona tried to drop out.

Fiona looked at Neil and blew out her cheeks. Neil had never seen her looking so dishevelled, and despite their complaints, he knew that they had thoroughly enjoyed themselves.

The time to leave for the airport the next day came round far too quickly for them all, and once there, the usual shaking hands, back slapping, kissing, and crying took place.

As Antoine shook Neil's hand, he said in a whisper.

"I think it is good for you both that perhaps you try for a baby, your Feefee she very much wants to have a family, Lysianne tells me this, and she knows these baby things very well."

Neil laughed and slapped Antoine on the back.

"We do try Antoine…all the time, maybe one will come."

After the plane had gone, they drove home and Fiona was very subdued, she was always like this when she said goodbye to Chantal. The two of them had a very strong bond, which could not have been stronger if they were related, but she cheered up no end when on getting home Neil gave her a surprise gift.

Fiona had taken quite a few photos of their friends, but more of Chantal than of the others. Neil had taken one especially good shot of her in the flower garden, into the city to be enlarged and framed. Fiona squealed with delight when he gave it to her, and flung her arms round him.

"You really are a lovely man," she told him, and insisted that he went into their garage for a hammer and nail. By the time he came back with them, she had already chosen a spot for it, on their bedroom wall facing the bed.

Every so often over the next few weeks Neil would see her standing in front of the picture with a strange look in her eyes. Whenever this happened, he would remember Antoine's words, and wondered if they would ever have a baby?

Maybe they should try and get away on the weekends more often, or even cut down the extra hours at the office and spend more time with her; he was at a loss as what to do for the best. The woman he loved was definitely not a happy lady.

63

Chapter Nine

Neil was the first person into the office that morning, and had just finished reading a letter in that morning's post, when his assistant young Don Thompson walked in. For some reason or other Neil, now aged twenty-nine always thought of twenty-four-year-old Don as a youngster. Maybe it was because he considered that he had had more experience of life than the younger man.

Don had been with Neil for a year and had proved an asset to both him and the company. A confirmed bachelor, he led a very private life and was not seen around much at all the endless social events held around the city. He had a pleasant enough personality and got on very well with Fiona and their close circle of friends. In fact, he spent so much time at their house these days he had almost become part of the furniture.

It was both convenient and comforting having Don as a colleague and a friend, because whenever Neil had to be away on business for one or two days, Don would come over and stay in the guest wing.

Crime had been steadily on the increase over the last few years, and after a couple of break-ins and a rape, not too far away from their home, and despite their elaborate state of the art security system, Neil felt happier knowing there was a man in the house in his absence.

They wished each other good morning, and Neil called over.

"I hope you haven't got any plans for the next few days Don. Short notice I'm afraid. We are off to Mozambique tomorrow, he said, waving a letter in the air.

"This is an invite from the Minister of Agriculture in Maputo. They are planning a massive irrigation system to try and get the sugar business back on its feet. They have asked me to come down and advise them…and I can bring an assistant, which is you. I'll ask Jean to book us on a flight tomorrow, so when you get home tonight, get packing."

They were only away for three days, and it was three days of hell.

The area the Mozambique Government had chosen for their new scheme had more mosquitoes than Neil had ever seen. There were dense clouds of them everywhere, and he was sure that if it had not been for the constant application of repellent, their bodies would have been dried out husks before the first day had ended.

Neil had hoped they would be able to dine out at least once. He was really looking forward to a nice big platter of the famous tiger prawns which abounded in the local coastal waters, cooked in a hot spicy piri piri sauce, it was a meal to die for, with a couple of glasses of vinho verde to round off the evening.

But this was not to be. There was only one place to eat, and that was in the flea-bitten hotel where they were staying, in what was laughingly shown on the map as a town. Neil was glad when the job was complete and had never been happier to get on a plane to go home.

One of the thousands of female Anopheline mosquitoes in Mozambique had decided to slake her thirst with Neil's blood, and despite him having taken all the necessary precautions, she had infected him, and the week after their return he had gone down with malaria.

Fiona was wakened in the early hours of the morning, by Neil threshing around in the bed complaining that he was freezing cold.

His teeth were chattering so much, that when he asked if she would she get him another duvet, she found it difficult to understand what he was saying, as soon as she did, she got up and went to the cupboard to fetch one. On her return, she found that Neil had tossed their duvet from the bed and was obviously in distress. His body and sleeping shorts were soaked with sweat, and he was throwing his head violently from side to side.

She went down to the lounge and phoned the emergency services for an ambulance, and an hour later Neil was in a hospital bed.

For a week it was touch and go, with him drifting in and out of consciousness. He would twist and turn so violently the nurse had to put up the side bars to prevent him falling out of bed.

He kept crying out, sometimes just unintelligible sounds and other times calling for Fiona. But it was when he just lay there staring at the ceiling, absolutely still, as if death had already claimed him that worried Fiona the most.

Neil did not seem to be responding to the usual drugs, and the doctor treating him decided they needed some sort of help…urgently.

The registrar said there was somebody new at the Sisters of Mercy Hospital he had heard about, apparently, he was from Mozambique where malaria was still endemic, and was reputed to be really good.

On the eighth day, Fiona was standing by Neil's bed holding his hand when the door opened. She looked up to see a man dressed in white come in, he smiled at her.

66

"Good evening Mrs Owens," and went on to explain that he had been asked to come in to give a second opinion on her husband's condition, and to see if he could help.

He asked her to sit down, which she did, and then he sat down next to her.

"Mrs Owens," he began, he paused and looked down at the clipboard he was holding. "Mrs Owens…or may I call you Fiona?"

Fiona nodded yes. He smiled and put his out hand and shook hers.

"I'm sorry Fiona, forgive me for not introducing myself first. My name is José Dos Santos, and I am a specialist in Tropical Medicine, especially in malaria. I have examined your husband's blood results, and as you already know, for some reason he is not responding to treatment. I believe he was recently in Mozambique, which would explain why the strain of malaria he has is familiar to me. I have suggested we now try a new drug that I have been using with excellent results."

He leant forward slightly and took one of her hands in his two.

"Fiona, I do not wish to alarm you but there is something I think you should know about your husband's condition."

Fiona's eyes widened with shock…what was she about to hear?

"On rare occasions malaria parasites undergo a radical change in the human body and become much more serious. When this……"

Fiona interrupted him.

"What exactly are you trying to say doctor?"

He looked at her for a few seconds before continuing.

"I'm afraid he now has cerebral malaria, which affects the brain…but please do not be too afraid, as I said, this new drug has worked wonders, now if you will excuse me, I have to go and arrange for the treatment to begin. Speed is very important now."

Fiona felt reassured at José's quiet air of confidence, but still spent most of her time at Neil's bedside, passing anxious nights dozing fitfully in the reclining chair, that José had arranged to be moved into the room, to make her more comfortable.

With Neil's phases of delirium alternating between hot and cold, she constantly had to get up, and either put more blankets over him, when his teeth were chattering like castanets, to taking them off again, and bathing his body with ice water as he shook with the fever, sweat draining from every pore.

She had refused assistance from the night nurse, saying Neil was *her* husband, and was *her* responsibility, but night after night of this was a drain on her, and exhaustion was beginning to wear her down.

Even though he was unconscious most of the time, and not fully aware of his surroundings, somehow Neil seemed to know that he was fighting for his life and battled against the malaria. Fiona was certain that if he had not been such a strong man, he would already be dead. But gradually, with the new drugs fighting the parasites in his bloodstream, plus his determination, he eventually turned the corner, and was at last on the mend.

Fiona woke early one morning before sunrise, worn out after three particularly exhausting nights, to hear her name being called. It was very faint, but it had been enough to waken her. She got up and switched on the bedside light.

Neil was looking up at her with a faint smile on his face.

"Hello darling," he whispered, "where have you been?"

She began to cry with happiness and kissed his dry cracked lips. He whispered again, and she had to bend over him to hear what he was saying.

"Could I have a drink of water please?"

She was so pleased to hear him actually asking for a drink, and even more so when after drinking just a few mouthfuls, he did not immediately bring it back up again. Until then he had not been able to hold down food *or* water, getting everything through an intravenous drip, and José had been concerned at possible kidney damage. Now here he was asking for a drink.

When José came into the room later, after hearing that Neil was now fully awake and talking, Fiona asked if she could speak to him outside the room for just a moment.

In the corridor she put hands on Jose's arms, stretched up and kissed him softly on the mouth.

"I just don't know how to thank you" she said…"I'm sure if you hadn't been here, Neil would have died."

68

"Fiona my dear," he said with a smile. "I told you not to worry, I am the best...but I must be honest, for a while we were all a little concerned, but now all is well."

Neil was really surprised when Fiona told him that he had had lots of visitors, including Duncan and Moira, Don and Jean from the office, and scores of get-well cards, also messages of concern from Antoine and his family.

"Sorry darling, I'm afraid I don't remember any of them, not even you, but I do know that I kept hearing your voice...but I just couldn't see you."

He began to make rapid progress towards a full recovery, and on his insistence, and that of José's, Fiona finally went home nights to sleep in her own bed. She was very reluctant to go, as she was still concerned about him. He looked dreadful, although she did not say that to him. His tan now replaced by an unhealthy pale colour, and he had lost an unbelievable forty pounds in weight, but she also was showing the signs of strain; it had been a terrible ordeal for the both of them.

On his discharge from hospital Neil was taken to the front door in a wheelchair pushed by José, he had become very embarrassed, but was told that he could not just walk out, it was Hospital Policy for patients to leave this way. He shook hands with the doctor who had virtually saved his life, and although he was very grateful for the care the man had given him, over the last few days Neil had become aware of something about him he was not comfortable with.

Fiona however thought he was the bee's knees and had already invited him to come over to the house.

"You must come over for dinner one evening José," she had said, "so we can thank you properly...and do bring your wife."

José had smiled at them both.

"Alas Fiona, I have not yet found a woman who would have me. Maybe you know of someone who would take pity on a lonely bachelor, especially one like me" His face had taken on the sort of forlorn expression that makes some women go weak at the knees, and men want to vomit.

Fiona looked at the young doctor with a quizzical expression on her face, thinking.

69

'How come a gorgeous creature like this has stayed single for so long? Those dark flashing eyes and sensual lips were out of this world.' "Oh, come now José...don't be so modest." Neil wondered when they had got on first name terms, because he was always referred to as Mr Owens.

José came to dinner twice, the first time alone, and the evening had been pleasant enough, even though the young doctor did most of the talking, with Fiona hanging onto every word.

He told them that he was the third and youngest son in a Portuguese family living in Mozambique. His father was a widower of some ten years, and that they owned a banana plantation of one hundred thousand acres. As he was leaving, Fiona had taken his arm, saying.

"You must come again José."

On the second occasion he was accompanied by a very pretty young blonde. Neil had thought she would look good on anyone's arm but was not the sort of girl you would take home to meet your mother.

For some obscure reason, Fiona had taken an instant dislike to the poor girl, and a couple of times had passed remarks that left Neil squirming in his seat. To give the girl her due, after a while, she began to give as good as she got, and after coffee, Neil had given José a look that clearly said, 'it's time to take her home!'

José had taken the hint, and they had left, this time without any future invitation from Fiona.

After they had gone, Neil asked Fiona about her uncharacteristic behaviour.

"What on *earth* got into you...I have never seen you like that before, just what did that poor girl do to upset you so much?"

Fiona gave a big sigh and sat down on the settee.

"I know darling, I'm sorry. She didn't do anything *wrong*, it was...I don't know. I just didn't like him bringing someone like *that* into my home."

Neil was not quite sure just what she meant by, 'someone like that,' but thought it prudent not to pursue the subject; she was still obviously upset about something.

Still not fit enough to go back to work, Neil spent his recuperation time at home either lying on a reclining chair on their back verandah, catching up on all the reading he previously never seemed to have time for, or down at the club watching the tennis and golf.

As time passed, he began to be concerned about his relationship with Fiona. She had become very moody of late, snapping at him without any valid reason, and sometimes he felt as if she would rather be in someone else's company than his. Her trips to town during the day, and sometimes for an hour or so on an occasional evening had become more frequent.

One evening after dinner he gently queried her absences. She became enraged.

"How *dare* you question my movements, you are driving me *mad*, being here all the time."

He tried to point out that he was not *there* all the time, as she put it, but before he could say any more, she stormed out the front door. He winced on hearing the driveway gravel flying as she roared away from the house.

His concern increased one day when she was out, while looking through mail he had asked Jean to send over, he found a large brown envelope.

Assuming it was something to do with work, he opened it. It contained pamphlets about adoption, fostering and even fertility testing, and was obviously for Fiona. She had never said anything to him about that, and wondered why? As he read, he began to wonder if her problem *was* perhaps frustration about wanting to have a baby; and how he could broach the subject. He resealed the envelope and put it on the hall table.

After three weeks of inactivity, with Fiona's increasing irritation with him, he disregarded his doctor's advice, and phoned Jean to say he would be in to work on Monday.

Chapter Ten

At nine a.m. on Monday morning when Neil entered his office, he was pleasantly surprised to find it overflowing with well-wishers from other departments, all wanting to welcome him back. After they had all gone, he said to himself, but unfortunately loud enough for Don and Jean to hear.

"I wouldn't mind a welcome like that at home."

They looked at each other, and Don shrugged his shoulders.

A few weeks passed and most things in his life seemed to be back to normal, he had regained all the weight he had lost, and his tan was back in place; his illness now far behind him. Work was going well and the only thing that he was concerned about was his relationship with Fiona. Things had certainly cooled off in the bedroom recently.

For a while after his clash with Mrs Anopheline Fiona had shown him much love and tenderness but that had since waned.' I don't know,' he wondered, 'just how does a man keep a woman happy?'

He had begun to have niggling thoughts that she may have struck up a friendship with some man, and he had a suspect in mind...*José*.

There was no evidence of anything going on, and Fiona had never invited him back again.

He looked over at Don; as a young bachelor he would probably mix with other men who might in turn socialise with José, or someone who knew him. He would speak to him some time, but not just yet, he would let things go on for a while, and he did not want to risk embarrassing anyone if there was no reason to.

One afternoon Neil came back to his office from a business lunch with three Japanese tycoons in the New Stanley Grill, extremely pleased with himself. He had managed to get them to sign a three-year contract for the installation and maintenance of a water supply irrigation system they wanted, on a fifty-thousand-acre vegetable farm they were developing on the shores of Lake Naivasha.

73

He went down the hall to spread the good news to the head of the engineering division and spent a couple of hours going over plans with him.

When he got back to the office he was still in a good mood and felt like celebrating. He looked at his watch and was more than surprised to see it was already five thirty. He looked over at Don who was busy beavering away at something or other on his desk; neither he nor Don had ever been clock watchers, but it was time to go.

"Stop what you are doing Don. We're going to have a couple of cold ones at the Long Bar."

"Certainly Master, whatever you say."

Even though it was early Friday evening the bar was already bursting at the seams, and the sound of thirty plus men all seemingly talking at the same time, made conversation difficult; sometimes, as the level rose, it became downright impossible.

There was the usual mixed bunch of merry makers, all at different levels of celebration, but apart from the hard core of drinkers who looked as if they had started their Friday night at lunchtime, and most likely had, the majority of them, like themselves, had only just arrived straight from the office grind, and were standing with their first glass of ice-cold Tusker lager in their hands.

Neil finally managed to catch one of the three hard working barmen's attention, ordered two Tuskers, and shrugged his way out of the throng along the bar with them. He looked at Don and nodded towards a vacant corner table.

After another beer, and half an hour later, Neil had to shout to be heard.

"I don't know about you Don, but I've had enough of this row. Do you fancy coming home with me and having dinner with us? Fiona has promised a nice pot roast for seven thirty. She always makes too much food, seems to think I'm still a growing boy, and you know she's always pleased to see you".

"Thanks Neil, but don't you think Fiona would like a bit of notice?"

"Nonsense!" Neil answered, still having to shout. "Come on; let's get out of here before I go deaf."

They set off with Don just ahead of him. Halfway home he was stopped by two cars and a small van stationary in the middle of the road, completely blocking his way. The police and a couple of breakdown trucks arrived while he was waiting in the queue of traffic, and it was thirty frustrating minutes before he was able to resume his journey.

As he had expected, Don's Peugeot 405 was already parked at the front of the house, and as he walked past it, without thinking, he felt the bonnet; it was only *just* warm, so Don must have been there for a while.

As he was putting his key into the front door lock, a metallic clang came from the rear of the house. He cursed under his breath, already knowing what he was going to find, and he was right.

The kitchen lights were on, and he could see the lid from their dustbin lying on the ground with bits of garbage around it. There was a sudden flash of movement as something small darted off into the bushes. He knew exactly what it was. A large swamp mongoose had recently taken up residence in their garden, which it considered its personal Tapas Bar. Neil replaced the lid and turned towards the kitchen.

Don and Fiona were standing sideways onto him, facing each other. Realising that they could not see him because of the reflection on the glass, he stood there watching; wondering what the hell was going on.

Don had obviously said something to upset Fiona, who never needed much of a spark to set off the temper that matched the colour of her hair ablaze. It was obvious by their body language that something was wrong. Don was red faced and looking decidedly unhappy. Fiona had one hand on his arm and appeared to be shouting at him.

'What on *earth* could the poor bugger have said to upset her,' he thought? 'The two of them normally got on well together'.

As he watched, Don left the room, leaving Fiona standing there, now with her hands covering her face. Neil stayed where he was silently watching. Finally, Fiona also hurried out of the room. She had no sooner disappeared than Neil heard Don's car start up.

He ran round to the front of the house to ask him what was wrong and arrived just in time to see the car disappear out onto the main road.

He went in through the still open front door and locked it behind him. Don certainly had left in a hurry. Fiona was in the lounge, staring at an oil painting above the fireplace of the two of them standing together, with Mt Kilimanjaro dominating the background.

On hearing his footsteps behind her, she turned and walked over to him. The expression on her face gave no indication at all as to what had just occurred, and he began to think it was really nothing at all, and that he would just let her bring it up if she wanted to. Even if she did not, he could ask Don about it on Monday.

Kissing him on the cheek, she said surprisingly cheerfully.

"Hello darling, pity…you've just missed Don."

"I *know*…I had invited him for dinner. What was all that about then?"

Fiona looked at him with a puzzled look on her face.

"All *what*?" she asked.

"I saw the two of you through the kitchen window, having what looked like a row…that's what! Now, what the hell is going on?"

Fiona's face blanched.

"Do you mean to say you have been *spying* on me?"

"Don't be stupid, of course I haven't. Why on earth would I want to do that? I was only round there because I heard the dustbin going over. It was that damned mongoose rooting around in the rubbish again. While I was there, I couldn't help but notice the two of you were having a thing."

"We weren't having a *thing* as you call it. And anyway, what exactly are you implying…by having a *thing*? If you must know, Don had just told me that he was going to invite Sally Rushworth to go with him to the Gala Ball at the Town Hall next week."

'What's the problem with that, he's not doing anything wrong? He's single, and free to ask whomsoever he likes out…that's no crime."

He could see that Fiona was working herself up into a fury. The warning signs were always when two red patches appeared on her cheeks.

76

"You have *always* been a blind fool…you never notice *anything*. You may not know it, but Sally has just parted from her boyfriend, and she desperately wants to get back with him. But that swine Don is trying to take advantage of her, just at the time she is most vulnerable.

Although I like him, you know what a womaniser he is. She is my best friend, and I don't want to see her hurt. So, I told him exactly what I thought of him.'

What she had said about Don was certainly true. He did have a bit of a reputation with the ladies. Since his arrival in Nairobi, his name had been linked to the name of more than one married lady, nothing that could ever be proved. Just unconfirmed rumours about this and that, but he certainly seemed to have a penchant for married ladies. 'Probably feels safer, just not wanting to commit to someone free,' he reasoned.

There was a story going around that Don, although not particularly good looking was rather generously endowed, that was probably the attraction.

Neil's face broke into huge smile as he thought about it. 'One out of two wasn't bad…the lucky dog!'

"What are you smiling at? It isn't funny!"

Neil wiped the smile from his face.

"Sorry darling, I was just thinking about that mongoose."

Fiona gave him a withering look.

"You bloody men are so insensitive to women's' feelings. I don't know why we put up with you. And seeing that *you* invited Don for dinner, but now he's gone, you can have dinner with the mongoose that you find so amusing, because I'm going to bed…goodnight, and don't wake me up!" She gave him another hard look and stormed out of the room.

Neil knew better than try and reason with her when she was in that frame of mind, so he accepted the situation, had pot roast a' la one, helped down by half a bottle of Cabernet Sauvignon, watched TV, showered and went to bed.

Fiona was fast asleep as he slipped under the duvet on their king size bed, if she wasn't she was giving a damn good impersonation.

She was lying on her back, looking so peaceful. He smiled, thinking of the difference between now and earlier, when she was

77

tearing him off a strip. Even without makeup she was a beautiful and highly desirable woman. He considered himself a very lucky man.

Propping himself up on one elbow alongside her, he was content with the simple pleasure of just watching her sleep. Now and then her eyelids would flutter, and he wondered if she was dreaming, and what, or about whom. 'Let's see what tomorrow brings,' he thought. If Fiona were running true to form, and she invariably did, by the morning, hopefully she would have forgotten they had even had a tiff...hopefully. Perhaps the weekend, would bring back the Fiona he loved so much.

Neil watched Fiona for a few more minutes, then leant over and gently kissed her forehead, then both her cheeks, she stirred slightly, and for a brief moment he thought she was going to wake up, which would definitely not be a good thing to happen. But she didn't.

He switched off his bedside light, eased himself carefully down onto his side and just before drifting off to sleep, he remembered that Don was supposed to be going with them.

He would just have to wait and see how Fiona was in the morning, when he raised the question as to whether she still wanted Don to accompany them. He tossed and turned for a while, his breathing became slower, before falling asleep.

Fiona turned over as quietly as she could and watched Neil's chest rising and falling until she was satisfied that he *really* was asleep. She got up, put on her robe, and tiptoed downstairs. She went through into the kitchen, put on the light, and made herself a cup of cocoa. She sat down next to the phone deep in thought, while she slowly sipped her drink.

She reached a decision, picked up the phone and dialled a number. She had chosen to use this particular phone, as it was furthest away from the bedroom.

The ringing tone went on for ages, and Fiona was just about to ring off when it when it stopped, and a male voice answered. Fiona's conversation lasted for just a few minutes, and she was smiling when she left the room; watched by a mongoose sitting on the top of the dustbin outside the kitchen window, just waiting for the   light   to   go   out.

Chapter Eleven

Neil owned a thirty-two-foot yacht which he kept permanently moored on Lake Naivasha. Originally the boat which had been built in Nairobi, and they had named *Fiona's Fancy*, was to be tested at Naivasha, and then shipped to Mombasa, but the lake was a beautiful setting, and after sailing there two or three times, they both fell in love with the place. With its backdrop of Longanot the extinct volcano, the crystal-clear waters, fringed by vast beds of waving papyrus and magnificent yellow barked fever trees, the lake was truly breathtaking. This was now a permanent mooring for *Fiona's Fancy.*

Apart from the setting, the real bonus to the lake was the bird life. Pink flamingos, pelicans, kingfishers, and the regal looking fish eagles. There were too many species for them to remember all their names; it was a veritable bird paradise.

They had their favourites, but the winner, hands down for both of them was without a doubt the fish eagle. To hear their calls echoing across the lake made the hair on the back of your neck stand up. It was totally African. And to actually see one swooping in from the top of the lakeside fever trees, snatching a fish from the surface with its wickedly long and sharp talons was a sight never to be forgotten, especially in the morning or the evening, when the sun low in the sky would catch the glint of the white chest and deep bronze belly feathers.

The owner of the Lakeside Hotel was an old school friend of Neil's, who in exchange for the use of the yacht himself now and again, looked after it and hauled it out of the water during the long rains season, when it was not in use.

Neil watched Fiona for a few more minutes, then leant over and gently kissed her forehead, then both her cheeks, she stirred slightly, and for a brief moment he thought she was going to wake up, which would definitely not be a good thing to happen. But she didn't.

He switched off his bedside light, eased himself carefully down onto his side and just before drifting off to sleep, he remembered that Don was supposed to be going with them.

He would just have to wait and see how Fiona was in the morning, when he raised the question as to whether she still wanted Don to accompany them. He tossed and turned for a while, his breathing became slower, before falling asleep.

Fiona turned over as quietly as she could and watched Neil's chest rising and falling until she was satisfied that he *really* was asleep. She got up, put on her robe, and tiptoed downstairs. She went through into the kitchen, put on the light, and made herself a cup of cocoa. She sat down next to the phone deep in thought, while she slowly sipped her drink.

She reached a decision, picked up the phone and dialled a number. She had chosen to use this particular phone, as it was furthest away from the bedroom.

The ringing tone went on for ages, and Fiona was just about to ring off when it when it stopped, and a male voice answered. Fiona's conversation lasted for just a few minutes, and she was smiling when she left the room; watched by a mongoose sitting on the top of the dustbin outside the kitchen window, just waiting for the light to go out.

Breakfast that morning was early, and even at six o' clock Fiona still looked stunning. She came to the table dressed in as she called it, her mariner's outfit, pale lilac trousers, and matching jacket, worn over a light blue silk shirt. Don's name had not come up and Neil thought it prudent to leave it that way.

He had decided to take the Range Rover this trip. Sometimes if there had been heavy rain the night before, the road down to the lake could be a bit tricky. Their last outing had been completely ruined, with most of the morning spent trying to get their Citroen convertible out of the mud.

The road down into the Rift Valley was one of Neil's favourites. The view was spectacular, especially from the car park at the first great horseshoe bend in the road, known to all the locals as the loop, and Neil always made it a point to stop there for a few minutes on the way down the escarpment.

Here they drank coffee fresh from their travel thermos, steaming in the cold morning air. Then they watched the rock hyrax's sunning themselves on the boulders that covered the steeply sloping side of the escarpment.

Two hundred feet below they could see dozens of the little creatures fluffing up their fur to let the early morning sun drive the night cold from their bodies.

As they watched, the tranquil scene below erupted into a stampede of terrified animals bolting to the safety of their holes.

Swooping out of the sun a Bateleur eagle twisted and turned, performing unbelievable manoeuvres to pluck one of the unfortunate hyraxes up in its talons. It gave a shriek of triumph as it winged its way back into the forest, with the limp form dangling pathetically below, where no doubt a pair of hungry fledglings were waiting impatiently for their breakfast.

The name Bateleur was derived from the French for acrobat. The bird certainly deserved its name, and even though Neil felt pity for the hapless animal, he had to admire the flying skills of the eagle.

This stop was especially poignant for Neil. Down below him on the almost vertical boulder covered slopes were the remains of five car wrecks. All of them either attempted insurance frauds, or genuine accidents, except for one.

What was now a distorted wreck of rusted metal had once been a sleek, powerful cream coloured Jaguar XK 120, the proud possession of John Palmer, a close friend of Neil's.

The wreck was a constant reminder to Neil and other of John's friends just how an enjoyable evening out with friends could so easily end in tragedy.

Neil's eyes misted over as his mind went back to that evening three years ago. They had all been out for a Saturday night dinner dance at Torr's Hotel, a very popular venue with the younger set. A party of twelve with one idea in their minds, to enjoy themselves, and that is just what they were doing.

Everything had been absolutely wonderful, lots of laughter and harmless fun, without the aid of too much alcohol.

At midnight, the band played Goodnight Ladies and the men all went off to get the ladies' coats from the cloakroom. Neil was making his way back to Fiona when he caught sight of John and his girlfriend Jenny having a blazing row.

He hurried over to try and calm things down and got there just as John stormed past him on his way out of the hotel, completely ignoring Neil saying.

"What's up John?"

That was the last time he was ever seen alive.

The first of the early morning visitors stopping at the loop, drove back to a nearby restaurant and phoned the police. An hour later they arrived with an ambulance. They never brought a tow truck as it was virtually impossible to recover any of the vehicles, just an ambulance to take away the shattered body or bodies; there were never any survivors.

The police report in the following Friday's edition of the East African Standard, concluded that from the evidence of the tyre tracks across the dirt surface of the car park, and the distance the car had travelled from the edge before it struck, the car must have been travelling at least sixty miles an hour, and no obvious attempt had been made to negotiate the corner. Therefore, the driver, a Mr John Templeton Palmer must have either been asleep at the wheel or he had committed suicide. The coroner after hearing the facts of the case ruled that it was suicide while the balance of the mind was disturbed.

Neil discovered later from Jenny, that the reason John had stormed off, was because she had told him

she wanted to end their relationship; she was in love with someone else, and that she was going home with him that evening.

All these years later, tears still came to Neil's eyes as he looked down at the wreck of his friend's car. What a dreadful waste.

The next stop was at the miniature Roman Catholic Church situated at the bottom of the escarpment. It had been built during the latter part of World War Two, by desperately home sick Italian prisoners of war, to commemorate the deaths of the prisoners who had died whilst constructing the road down into the Rift Valley.

It was a beautiful little church with a graceful steeple. Inside there was room for a congregation of about twenty. There were never any Sunday services, and the only prayers were offered up by passing motorists like themselves, who delayed their journey for whatever personal reasons they had.

Neil always stopped at the church, because like the hapless Italian POW's, his parents had also died on the escarpment.

They had been returning to Nairobi on a Sunday evening, after a weekend with friends in Nakuru. His father had been piloting the Piper Cherokee, and although he was a skilled pilot, with many years of flying experience he had misjudged his altitude, while flying through dense cloud obscuring the top of the escarpment.

The small plane had plunged into the hillside, killing them both instantly. It was truly a tragedy, because the next day when the search party found the wreck, they could see that if the plane had been a mere fifty feet higher, they would have flown over, and landed safely at Nairobi's Wilson Airport.

As Neil knelt at the foot of the small altar, he imagined the voices of the Italians praying for their loved ones joining his, and he felt his parents were not alone.

Fiona invariably stayed outside the church. She had never met his parents and felt this was a personal moment for him that should not be intruded upon.

It only took another thirty minutes to reach the Lakeside Hotel car park, and Neil did not know whether he felt surprised, relieved, or disappointed to see Don's car parked there. There was no sign of Charlie and Sue, the friends they were to be sailing with, but Neil knew they would be along in no time at all; sailing was their life. Fiona said nothing and followed him into the hotel.

The place seemed deserted, but Neil knew that Bill and Cathy, their friends that owned the hotel would have been up for hours, making sure the guest's breakfasts would be ready on time. It was an extremely popular hotel, always full at weekends, and if you wanted to stay it was advisable to book well in advance.

He also knew that even at that early hour, the bar on the front verandah would be open. It was a popular bar, ideally set with views overlooking the lake, which was only about one hundred and fifty yards away; actually, the distance to the shore varied by fifty yards or so each year, depending how much rain they had.

Although small, the bar was well stocked, and surprisingly, when the barman was not on duty, it was run on an honour system. Which meant if you wanted a drink when the barman was not there, you helped yourself, and then wrote your name, and what you had taken, in the book kept on the bar counter. It was very popular with the people living in the area, who frequently dropped in to take advantage of a friendly watering hole, and Bill reckoned it was a good sales gimmick. Thirsty locals knew they could pop in and get a drink at any time.

Neil had asked Bill once about losses when people forgot to list all their drinks. He had laughed.

"It all comes out even in the end Neil. Now and again one of the regulars will pop in looking a little red faced after a good night *before*, and because he'd remembered the next morning about two or three drinks he'd forgotten to sign for, guilt would make them add a few more onto their tab, so nobody really lost out. So...*swings and roundabouts."*

There were two elderly couples sitting at the same table on the verandah, drinking coffee and gazing wistfully out over the lake, and one solitary figure perched on a bar stool nursing a glass of beer. It was Don. He was obviously lost in thought because when Neil tapped him on the shoulder, he jumped and spilt half his beer.

"Didn't know if you were going to be here or not today Don, but I'm glad you are." Neil whispered into his ear.

Fiona had taken a seat at a nearby table and appeared not to have noticed that it was Don at the bar. But Neil knew she had. 'That business about Sally really had upset her,' he thought. He looked over at her, to see her busily scrimmaging through her handbag.

"You're obviously okay for a drink Don......or what's left of it, I'd better see what Fiona wants."

They went over and sat down.

"Look who I found propping up the bar Fiona."

Fiona looked up and said with more than a hint of sarcasm in her voice.

"Hello Don...nice of you to come...although I'm sure you have other friends you'd rather be with."

Neil squirmed slightly embarrassed at her cutting remark, and Don did not look too happy either.

Fiona said she would like a coffee, and while Neil waited at the counter for someone to come from the kitchen to take his order, he glanced over to see Don and Fiona talking, or at least Fiona was talking, with Don still looking very unhappy.

Neil took the coffees over to the table and put them down, now feeling a little irritated at what he was now considering a childish situation. He stood there looking at them.

"For God's sake, will you two please pack it in. This whole thing is beginning to get on my bloody nerves. And if you aren't going to snap out of it, we might as well go home now. I know Charlie and Sue are not going to be impressed with the vibes you two are giving off. Like me, they are coming to have a good day's sailing. So, let's call a truce shall we."

Fiona looked at him for a few seconds, and then her face lit up with a smile that disarmed him completely.

"OK darling, just for you, and Charlie and Sue, I'll forgive him, but he had better be nice to me."

Don looked like a schoolboy that had just had his pocket money reinstated.

While they were talking, their two guests arrived and joined them, accompanied by Bill. Greetings were exchanged all round and plans for the day's sailing began.

"I've put a cooler box full of iced Tuskers in the galley for you lads," Bill whispered to Neil, "and a couple of bottles of bubbly for the ladies. I presume you've brought your own grub, if you haven't, I can get the chef to rustle you up something quickly."

"Thanks Bill, we've brought everything we need, except for the drinks, but thanks for the offer."

Bill nodded his head towards the lake.

"She's clean and ready to go, and I think you may have the whole lake to yourself today, there's some sort of regatta going on at Lake Elementeita this weekend, and everybody seems to be heading that way. Not that I mind, we have our hands full with two coach loads of German bird watchers here. Can you believe, bird watchers, all the way from Bavaria, just to visit my little lake?"

Halfway to the dock Neil suddenly caught hold of Don's arm and pulled him to a stop.

"I don't believe it...what the hell is he doing here?"

Don looked around, wondering who Neil was talking about.

"Who do you mean Neil?"

"Over there coming through the trees. That damn José, I know I owe him, but there is something about him that makes me feel uneasy; and what a coincidence him being here today. It'll be interesting what he says.'

Don turned as Neil had been speaking and could see someone coming towards them from the car park. It could not have been more obvious that he was pretending he hadn't seen them, and Don couldn't help a snort of disbelief when he turned, as if he was going to return to the car park but had then suddenly noticed them.

He called out hello and walked briskly over to them.

"Hey," he said with a smile. "Fancy meeting you here, what are doing...going to have a picnic?"

Neil turned away in disbelief. Seeing they were all dressed in sailing gear, complete with life jackets slung over their shoulders, it was a pretty safe bet, what they were there for.

"No José, we're going sailing, but what brings you here today?"

"Well really, I just came to see the lake, one of the doctors at the clinic brought in some photos the other day, and it looked so beautiful I thought I would see for myself. Anyway, have a great day sailing."

He turned and had just begun to walk away when Fiona called out.

"Wait...José.' She turned and took Neil's arm. "There's plenty of room on the boat "Neil, José, could come with us, then he would really see the lake; where better than from a boat."

This really put Neil on the spot; he turned and looked at Charlie and Sue, to get some indication as to how they felt about someone who was a stranger to them joining them for the day, but nobody objected, so he introduced him to them.

José was wearing a track suit and trainers, with a waterproof jacket draped over one shoulder.

"Well, seeing you are almost dressed for the part I suppose it will be alright." Neil said trying to sound as if he meant it."

"Hang on Neil," Don said, it won't be safe, he hasn't got a life jacket."

Fiona swung towards with a glint in her eye.

"That's no problem. We have a couple of spares on board."

They all stood looking from one to the other, as if waiting to see who was going to speak next.

"That's it then," Neil said. He stood back allowing the others to board, with José last on. As he passed him, Neil had a feeling of suspicion begin to germinate in his mind.

They stowed all their gear safely away, and Charlie and Neil hoisted the mainsail and jib. With the wooden jetty jutting out thirty metres into the lake it was possible for Neil to sail directly out into open water without having to use the outboard.

There had been a couple of minutes of excitement when they arrived at the dock. A half-grown hippo dining on the water lilies in the shallows alongside the jetty had panicked on seeing them, and ploughing its way out to the deep water, had created a bow wave that rocked the boat and drenched the two girls, much to the men's amusement. They made sure that they didn't show it though, as the girls hadn't seen the funny side at all. But in no time the warm sun had dried them out and they soon looked none the worse for wear.

Fiona and Sue had been friends since their schooldays, as had Neil and Charlie. They were fortunate in that the four of them got on really well together and made a point of maintaining their strong bond of friendship by regular social outings which included sailing at least once a month. Neil always said.

"No use having a lovely boat if you hardly ever use it."

It was a beautiful day with a good steady wind blowing from the north. They crisscrossed the lake several times and decided to have their lunch on Crescent Island.

Because of the shallows, they would have to use the dinghy which Charlie had inflated, to get ashore, and now it bobbed along behind them.

Once on the island, Don volunteered to take the dinghy back to the yacht to fetch the food and drink while Charlie and Neil spread a groundsheet for them to all to sit on.

While they worked, José just sat on a rock chatting to Fiona and Sue. Charlie drew Neil's attention to them, asking.

'Bit of a ladies' man is he then?'

Neil had not taken his eyes off José since they had arrived, and unable to think of a suitable answer, just nodded.

They enjoyed a good lunch, and a bit too much wine was drunk.

The decision was for them to have a little siesta, just to be on the safe side, before setting off. Even with the water on the lake as calm as it then was, violent storms could suddenly destroy the day, and it would be foolish to take risks after having a few drinks.

José, who not drunk anything alcoholic said he was going to walk around the island, and asked Fiona if she would care to join him. She looked at Neil as if for approval, and decided that the look in her husband's eyes indicated a *no*. She refused, saying she needed a lie down. José just shrugged and walked off without commenting.

Don said he was going out to sit on the boat and fish, Neil could see by the look on his face the real reason was that he was just feeling spare, and out of it. He felt sorry for him, he really should try and get a regular girlfriend, maybe Sally would be a good thing for him, and perhaps he would try and get them together.

After an hour of dozing and not able to settle, Neil got to his feet. The others were fast asleep, with Charlie was lying on his back snoring away. Neil felt he needed a swim to clear the cobwebs away and stripped down to the swimming trunks he always wore under his trousers when sailing. He swam around for a while and then over to the boat.

Don had given up pretending to fish, and was lying stretched out on the deck, catching some sun. He got up and handed Neil up onto the boat.

Don went below deck and came back with a couple of opened beers. He gave one to Neil and they clinked bottles together. They sat quietly for a while, just enjoying the day, and Neil decided to say something.

89

"Don I'm going to tell you something that is just between the two of us…okay?"

"Sure, boss man, I'm all ears," Don said with a laugh trying to lighten the moment, as he could see Neil had something serious on his mind.

"I hate to say this, but I think Fiona may be cheating on me."

"*No way Neil*…not Fiona. Are you serious?"

"Unfortunately, yes I am."

"Have you anyone in mind?"

Neil nodded towards the shore.

"Jose…I know the man saved my life, and I have no real reason to suspect him, but something just doesn't feel right."

Don stared at Neil for a few seconds.

"Well, I have only met him a couple of times, but I must say I didn't take to him right from the first time I met him at the hospital."

"As a friend Don I am going to ask you a big favour, and I will understand if you say no. Could you just keep your ears open, and if you hear anything at all, let me know?"

"'I sure will Neil, anything for a friend."

The sun was still shining but now there were clouds scudding across the sky, driven by a wind that had increased quite a bit and veered slightly, which was never a good sign on that lake.

The two men rowed back to the island and ferried the others out to the yacht. Once they were all back on board, they hoisted the sails and set off. Their return trip was a bit hairy, and the girls stayed out of the way below deck with José. With the main sheet stretched as tight as a drum, they were moving across the lake at a fair rate of knots.

A few minutes into their journey Neil told Don to join the girls, that he and Charlie could manage; Don had very little sailing experience and would just get in the way if things became livelier than they already were.

No sooner had he gone below, when the weather, always unpredictable showed just how fickle it could be. With half a mile to go before they could dock, and without warning, they found themselves almost becalmed, with just enough wind for them to make headway. Looking back, Neil could see the squall behind them slowly moving away from them back across the lake.

90

From where he stood on deck, Neil could see Fiona and Don down in the cabin talking together.

They seemed to be having an intense conversation and were certainly not arguing.

"Thank God for that," Neil said to himself, "normality again." He hated confrontations and unpleasant situations.

Don came up from the cabin and made his way over to Neil.

"That guy is unbelievable, he may be a damn good doctor but his chat up line stinks, and the girls are lapping it up. I had to come out and get some fresh air. I can tell you Neil, it will be a pleasure keeping an eye on him."

They docked, lowered the sails, and carried all their gear up to the hotel. Bill was waiting for them at the bar on the front verandah. He told Neil that he would put the boat to bed, which was always a blessing.

"Cathy and I would like you all to be our guests for dinner tonight. We've made good profit courtesy of our German friends this weekend, and we want to celebrate."

José made his apologies to everyone and said unfortunately there was an appointment he had to keep at the hospital. He thanked them all for a wonderful day and left. As he walked away, several pairs of eyes followed him, each pair seeing him in a different light.

At the dinner table Don sat between Fiona and Sue; with José gone the atmosphere seemed more relaxed, and the three of them were having a great time, and the dinner was a great success.

Reluctantly they all said their thanks and goodbyes and made their way out to the car park. Neil noticed that Fiona kissed Don warmly on both cheeks, which was a good sign, before she got into the Range Rover.

Fiona must have found the day tiring because she was fast asleep before they hit the main road and stayed asleep until he gently nudged her awake outside their front door.

She refused his offer of a nightcap.

"No thanks I'm ready for bed," she said with a yawn.

Neil looked up from cleaning his teeth. In the mirror above the wash hand basin, he could see Fiona's reflection. She was standing sideways on to him, completely naked, in front of her full-length mirror brushing her hair.

With each stroke of the brush her head tilted back, showing to full advantage the graceful outline of her neck and features. Just the simple act of brushing her hair gave such a picture of vulnerable innocence that he felt almost guilty, as if he were intruding on something completely private.

He carried on brushing his teeth, and when he looked up again, she was just slipping a negligee over her head. The pale apricot negligee, so sheer it was almost an angel's breath floated down over her body, then she turned and disappeared from view.

She was sitting up in bed reading when he came through, and looked up at him, her eyebrows lifting slightly as she saw that he was wearing the pyjama bottoms he had bought as a joke on one of their holidays in Bali.

They were an absolute riot of every colour you could imagine. Jumbled scenes of half-naked girls with hibiscus flowers in their hair, cavorting madly around bougainvillea bushes, and palm trees infested with birds of paradise. Pyjamas from hell she had called them, designed by a madman.

He had only worn them once while they were there, and on their return home, had bundled them into the back of the bedroom cupboard, where they had remained ever since.

His decision to wear them to bed that night was just to try and cheer her up. Her mood since returning that evening from the lake had been strange, almost as if she were somewhere else.

The sight of him standing there however, did make her smile, and seeing that made him feel a little less foolish.

"I just thought you might like a laugh, you seem a little down this evening. I thought we all had a great time at the lake. Is there something wrong?"

"No Neil, nothing is wrong. Just a bit too much sun I think, and something girlie you would not understand…don't worry. I will be fine after a good night's sleep. Just come to bed. But for goodness's sake take those ridiculous things off."

Neil went into their dressing room, and when he came back out with his usual night wear, a pair of plain cotton shorts, she looked up.

"That's more like it. I think we will have to take a photo of you in those other ghastly things, and then we will burn them on the back lawn. I have no idea why you ever bought them."

"Fiona! If I remember correctly, it was your idea to buy them. You said they would be fantastic to wear if we ever got invited to a pyjama party. And thank God we haven't.*"*

Neil settled his head onto his pillow, his mind and body, but especially his body, now remembering other nights. Fiona was wearing his favourite perfume, Hawaiian Ginger, the one perfume that really turned him on; and she knew it.

He looked over at her and breathed in a lungful of her perfume, his mind full of romance and expectation. As he did so, she put down her book, leant over.

"Goodnight darling, sleep well,*"* kissed him on the cheek, and turned onto her other side.

It was a good few seconds before Neil realised his hoped for a night of passion was not to be, but he still could not believe it.

'Just how does a woman's mind work?*'* he thought. A fantastic day out on that beautiful lake, and what do I get? 'Goodnight darling, sleep well'. He picked up his book from the bedside table, but before opening it he turned, and said quietly to the back of Fiona's head.

"And goodnight to you as well my darling.*"*

After a few pages he lost interest in the story, his mind full of confusion as to what he should do about trying to confirm his suspicions that perhaps Fiona was seeing José. He mulled over a few options before deciding on a plan of action, then switched off his lamp and went to sleep content with his decision.

Chapter Twelve

It was Thursday morning, and Neil was more than glad the week was almost over; a week that had been full of frustration for him. He had worked out a sort of scheme to try and ease his suspicions about Fiona, but the more he thought about it, the more complicated and impractical it seemed to get. But now he felt ready and was about to put phase one into action that morning.

"Before I forget darling," Neil had called out from the front door on his way to work. "I have to drive up to Fort Hall today. They are having some big problems at the Chania pumping station with the new pumps we commissioned last week, and they would like me to try and sort out the problem. I won't be home until about nine, so don't get dinner for me. I'll get something on the way back."

"Okay," she called out as she came through from the kitchen "Thanks for letting me know."

Neil had been puzzling for ages as to how Fiona maybe getting in touch with whoever...if there really was someone. She probably had some intricate way of contacting him; and maybe that was where she went on her trips out in the evening. When all she said was, 'I'm just popping out to see one of my friends', which up until then, Neil had automatically assumed was a female friend; now he was not so sure. If it was José, was she meeting him at the hospital? She was never gone long enough for her to drive out his flat, he lived six miles the other side of town. Was she perhaps leaving messages somewhere? This morning he was going to find out for sure if she was, and if so, where.

He drove out of the gate as normal, turned onto the main road, and one hundred yards further down swung into the driveway of a neighbour's house, and parked up behind a large stand of bamboo, just where he could see his own drive. The owners of the house were away on holiday, he knew this, because they had left their house keys with him in case of emergency.

He sat and waited patiently, and not in vain. Fifteen minutes later Fiona drove out in her bright yellow Audi and headed off towards the city.

Neil let a couple of cars go past before he joined the morning traffic! which was heavy enough to keep him out of her sight, but light enough for him to stay with her.

She turned left at the Khoja Mosque down Government Road, and then right onto Delamere Avenue.

Neil followed her cautiously all the way down the avenue. The traffic had increased considerably now they were in the city, but because of the distinctive colour of her car, he was easily able to keep her in sight. Three cars ahead he saw her left indicator was flashing, showing that she intended turning into the Post Office car park. He slowed down a little until she was well into the parking ground, before driving in himself.

Fiona parked and walked off down a path towards the District Commissioner's office. Neil jumped from his car and ran quickly across the car park at an angle to the path she had taken, towards the front of the building.

He peeped round the corner of the building, just intime to see Fiona putting something into the open end of a metal pipe behind a mahogany bench, before walking back to her car.

Neil stayed where he was for a few more minutes to allow her to get well away, and then walked over to the bench.

He had not been at all happy at spying on the woman he loved, but drastic times needed drastic measures, and he consoled himself with the thought that whatever he did, it would be for the good of them both in the end.

He walked over and looked into the open end of the pipe. He could see a folded over piece of paper, which he took it out and read.

The note was unsigned, and no names were mentioned. It just said. 'Can't wait to see you.'

He put the note back into the pipe and returned to his car, where he sat for a while deep in thought, with an ache in his chest that threatened to overwhelm him. He took a deep breath…so she *was* seeing someone.

Time to face the facts my boy. At least he now knew how they made contact, but who was the man? He wondered if he checked for a message every day, or did she have some way of letting him know there was one waiting for him?

Neil arrived at his office half an hour late that morning, which was very unusual for him. He walked into the office and paused at Jean's desk.

"Good morning, sorry I'm late……traffic problems, any messages for me?"

"Not so far," she answered.

'I'm driving up to Fort Hall today," he told her. Giving her the same story as he had Fiona, so if anyone else phoned for him, they would be told that was where he was.

"They called me early this morning at home, so it must be something urgent. Don't try and contact me because we will be out on the line all day."

His assistant Don called out a cheery,

"Good morning boss man" as Neil passed his desk. He was currently working on the construction of a new industrial complex that was near completion. He had been almost pathetically grateful when Neil had turned it over to him. It was a major project which Neil would normally have done himself, but he felt the young man showed promise, and needed the show of confidence.

There was nothing of importance in his mail, so after saying goodbye and saying he would see them the next day, he set off for Fort hall.

Luckily for Neil there *were* a few minor problems at the pumping station that was he able to help with, and the time passed surprisingly fast. He made a leisurely return to Nairobi, after stopping briefly at the Red Lion in Ruiru for a beer and a light snack at five thirty.

Neil had assumed the man his wife may be seeing was a businessman with normal office hours, so while at the Red Lion, he took a chance, and phoned Fiona to say he had finished early, and would be home at six, and that he had something very important to show her. On hearing his message, she began to splutter something about having to go out, but he cut her off in mid-sentence.

"Sorry dear I've run out of time and change…see you," and put the receiver down.

That should hopefully prevent her from keeping her rendezvous, although he chose not to dwell on just what he would do if she did turn up.

At exactly six forty-five he was parked in the Post Office car park, more than ready for whatever may happen.

He parked his car as close to the bench as he could, locked it, and made his way over to it.

He felt surprisingly relaxed, knowing that in a few minutes, he would know for sure the identity of whoever she was meeting, thus, ending weeks of frustrating speculation once and for all.

Standing in the shadows behind the bench Neil checked his watch. The time was exactly five past seven. He felt the prickles of concern, had they somehow been in touch already, thus neutralising his plan?

He shuffled his feet impatiently and at that moment noticed a figure hurrying towards him from the direction of the car park. He leaned further back into the shadow of the Jacaranda tree.

The nearest streetlamp was fifty or more feet away at the edge of the car park, and behind whoever it was approaching, so Neil was not able to see any facial features of the man coming towards him, but the outline did look vaguely familiar.

97

It was not until the man actually turned towards the bench and bent forward to take the note from the pipe, that even with the faint light from the car park, Neil was able to see the man's face clearly.

He could hardly believe his eyes on seeing who it was. Never in a million years would he have guessed his identity.

The viper in his nest was no other than Don…his so-called friend. And to think I actually asked him to spy on José, he must have had a bloody good laugh about that…the *bastard!*

Don's name had once popped into his mind as a suspect, but he had immediately dismissed the idea as being absolutely ridiculous. Now he knew who, but how on earth did he know when there was a message waiting for him?

He stood there hardly daring to breathe as he watched Don take out a lighter, which he flicked into life, so he could read the note; he read it quickly, then burnt it.

Neil stayed silently in the shadows, just watching, his heart thumping.

Don began to walk up and down in front of the bench impatiently looking at his watch every so often; obviously angry that Fiona had not turned up, then turned to sit down.

Neil stepped silently forward, and before Don's backside had touched the seat, Neil had wrapped his right arm round his throat, in a choke hold, and pulled him back as hard as he could, gripping him until he passed out.

He laid him out along the bench, tied his hands and feet together, hoisted his inert body over his shoulder and carried him back to the car park. He unlocked the boot, dropped Don into it, got in behind the steering wheel, and drove away.

He let out a great sigh of relief. It had gone much better than he had thought it would. His heart was pounding, a mixture of exertion and excitement.

He had already decided that if he found out who the mystery man was, he would take him somewhere secluded and hide him until he decided what to do next; and he knew just the place; one of the inspection chambers he had designed.

He drove to the one he had chosen; it was perfect for his plan.

He lifted his still unconscious passenger out and laid him on the ground. Next, he entered the code on the combination padlock and swung the grill open.

He dragged Don over, threw the holdall he had taken from the boot into the chamber, tied a length of nylon rope under Don's armpits, and lowered him to the floor. He clamped a torch on to the grill and directed the beam downwards, then climbed down.

The first thing Neil did was to look at the inspection report sheet that was attached to one of the valves. The valves had been checked the previous day, which meant the chamber would not be visited for another thirteen days.

He turned Don onto his back and untied the ropes. Next, he undressed him completely; even taking his shoes and socks, wallet, and watch. He put everything into the holdall and threw it up out of the chamber.

He felt not the slightest bit of pity as he looked down at the man who had caused so much unhappiness and turmoil in his life. He turned to go, and for one moment was tempted to give the still unconscious Don a goodbye kick, but as he wouldn't feel it, there was no point.

He checked around the chamber to make sure there was nothing left to link him in any way to the scene, in the unlikelihood of someone finding Don before his plan was complete. Satisfied that the place was clear, Neil climbed out, replaced the grill, and locked it.

With phase one successfully completed with no hitches at all. Neil was more than pleased with his evenings work.

Seeing Don's face as he read the note had really shocked him. He was going to be hard put not to let Fiona know anything that would make her suspicious. It would have been bad enough if he had not recognised the man's face, but to see the face of someone he had considered a friend, was almost unbearable.

Neil drove into town and stopped behind the Municipal market. He got out of the car and took the holdall out of the boot and over to a row of dustbins.

He distributed everything amongst five different bins, but before throwing the trousers in, he took out Don's bunch of keys, and smiled as he thought of the looks on the faces of the homeless people that he knew would be ferreting through the bins first thing in the morning. Especially those who found the shoes and the watch, Don always wore imported Italian shoes, and the watch was a gold Rolex.

He drove home slowly, deep in thought. Finding out it was Don had affected him far more than he thought it would. A stranger would have been bad enough… but *Don*! And now he had him, what was to do with him. He decided that he would leave him there for a few days, let him wonder what had happened, where was he, and who had brought him there.

Reaching home, he was still no nearer deciding what line to take with Fiona. Maybe he should play it by ear. There was no point in confronting her just yet; he would leave it until he decided exactly what he intended to do.

Fiona eating her dinner when he went into the house. He could see she was furious.

"Neil how could you?" she shouted at as soon as he walked in the room. "You said you were going to be here at six…an hour and a half ago. I was supposed to pop out to collect something, but it's too damn late now. You could at least have phoned again telling me you were still going to be late.

"Sorry dear, I ran out of change, still, no harm done, I'm here now."

"Well, I hope you have had something to eat, because I only made a snack for myself."

"No problem darling, I ate at the Red Lion."

"And just what was so important you had to show me, that you wanted me to be here when you got home?"

Neil reached into his jacket pocket and produced a brochure which he showed her. It had been in his pocket for a few days, just waiting for the right time.

"I have booked us in at Amboselli for a week, starting next Monday, it will be great to get away for a few days."

"Well, I hope you enjoy being there by yourself, because I won't be with you. Now I am going to bed. Don't wake me up!" She slammed the door as she went out.

The next day, Neil had been at his desk for only half an hour when Jean approached him.

"Don hasn't come in yet, which is unusual for him, do you think he might be sick?"

"I was going to wait until you were all here," Neil said, and explained that Don had called him the previous evening, telling him his father had phoned from Cape Town, with the news that his mother was seriously ill, and that he was needed there.

He asked Jean to please fill in the annual leave register saying that Don had been granted a month's compassionate leave.

He went out of the office later and came back with a smile on his face; another part of his plan completed.

That evening, Fiona complained of a splitting headache and went off to bed.

"Your headache is nothing like the one your boyfriend has my dear," Neil said to himself as she left the room.

Thankfully, she was asleep when he went up, because for the first time in their married life he did not particularly want her company.

The weekend passed quickly, with them uncharacteristically doing nothing at all other than lying around the house sipping drinks and   reading.

Chapter Thirteen

On the second day of Don's incarceration his name was finally brought up at the dinner table by Fiona. In a very casual tone.

"Oh, by the way darling, Sally Rushworth phoned me this afternoon, apparently she has been

trying to ring Don at home but can't get an answer. She asked me if I would speak to you, is he away somewhere?"

Neil looked across at her, his fork halfway to his mouth feigning a look of surprise.

"Obviously, Sally hasn't phoned the office, or Jean would have told her about him."

"*Told her what?*" Fiona asked.

Neil explained about Don being called away to Cape Town, because of his mother's illness and that he had taken a month's leave.

"You never mentioned it."

"Since when have I ever talked about Don's private affairs?" He had not really meant to put it that way, but it was rather appropriate. "And I just didn't think to mention it to you, no doubt we'll hear from him soon."

Fiona looked up at Neil who was now concentrating on his newspaper, his explanation certainly explained the mystery as to why Don had not turned up.

Hearing about his sudden departure left her with mixed emotions. Anger came first. Leaving just like that without letting her know, which he could easily have done, then a strange feeling of relief.

In the beginning, Don's attention to her had been flattering, and the intrigue of meeting him for a few snatched moments in the dark were like something out of a novel. Thinking back to it all now she realised that it was rather like the sort of story that schoolgirls swooned over.

Nothing had happened between them, alright they had kissed a couple of times, but that was all, and what was a kiss really, if there was no love.

She knew that he wanted to sleep with her. He had asked her several times if they could maybe go away somewhere for the night, but she had never intended to go that far, and told him so; but she had not told him that she regarded it as just a bit of harmless romantic fun.

Fiona had bumped into Sally recently at The Thorn Tree, and they had had coffee together. Sally told her that Don was becoming a real nuisance. He had tried it on with her, in fact he had started to become a real pest, phoning her at work, and at home, asking her to go out with him. But Sally was still too much in love with her ex-boyfriend and would have nothing to do with him. She went on to tell her that Don had a really bad reputation with other men's wives and girlfriends, and it was only a matter of time before some husband caught him out.

Fiona was shocked, that was a side of Don she had been completely unaware of.

Neil folded his newspaper and put it down. He stood up and came round to her, leaning over he gave her an unusually warm kiss as he told her he was going.

She watched him leaving and realised just how foolish she had been, Neil was worth a thousand Dons.

She now knew she had been giving him a hard time recently and was determined she was going to make up for it, he was a wonderful husband, and despite her foolishness they were very much in love.

The only reason she had encouraged Don was because she was feeling as if life was passing her by, with no baby to love and care for. From now on there would be no more lying and sneaking around, which in retrospect had always made her feel uncomfortable and ashamed; but that was all in the past now, with this decision made, her feeling of relief was even greater, and it felt as if a millstone had been suddenly lifted off her back.

Neil left Don for three days before going back again to see him. This would give him plenty of time to sweat it out, worrying as to what was going to happen to him, and who had put him there.

On the morning of the third day, he told Jean that he had a doctor's appointment but would not be away long.

In the boot of Neil's car was a holdall with sandwiches and a plastic bottle of water. He parked next to the grill and got out. He shone the torch down into the chamber and could see Don lying motionless on his back. He again deliberately let the grill drop back with a clang, just to give Don something more to worry about. He would have no way of knowing…was this a rescue or was he going to be killed?

Neil raised him into a sitting position and put the plastic bottle of water to his lips. He tried to gulp it down, but Neil restrained him, only allowing it to dribble out, until he was able to drink properly. Still holding him propped up, he gave Don the sandwiches, which were devoured in seconds. Neil then lowered him back down onto the floor and stood up.

Don had made no effort to speak or move, he just lay there looking up at Neil, and then he croaked a feeble.

"Hello!"

Still silent, Neil stood motionless just looking down at the man who had nearly destroyed his life. He felt no pity in his heart as he remembered the anguish he had suffered because of him. He moved slightly, and light must have fallen on his face, because a look of horror came on Don's face as he realised who had brought him here and why.

Don began begging and pleading for Neil to let him go. The words just tumbled out of his mouth in an almost mindless babble, the ravings of a near lunatic. Neil just stood there stony faced without saying a word, until Don stopped, then he turned and began climbing up.

Halfway up Don suddenly lunged across the chamber and jumped upwards, scrabbling frantically at Neil's legs. He managed to catch hold of one of them just as Neil was about to clear the top. With one swift kick with his free leg Neil kicked Don in the face, sending him crashing back down to the floor. Without even at a look at his prisoner, he locked the grill and left. The final part of his plan was to be carried out the next day.

Neil phoned Jean in the morning to say he would not be in that day, without explaining why, after all, he was the boss.

He found Don sitting with his back to the far wall and couldn't help smiling when he saw that he had a 'beaut' of a black left eye, with a small cut, on his cheek.

This time Neil had brought with him a holdall containing among other things, sandwiches, a bottle of water, a complete set of clothing, and a pair of shoes and socks.

It must have rained sometime during the night, and Don had used the rainwater falling through the grill to wash his body. He had been using the drain as a toilet and the rainwater had flushed it clean. The chamber and Don both now smelled a little fresher than on his last visit.

Neil waited while Don ate his food and drank his water. He stood there silently watching until Don had finished, and then took back the plastic bottle.

Don seemed to have become more rational and only asked the once, but still in a whining voice for Neil to let him go.

"I promise I won't say anything to anyone…I *promise*."

Neil put down the holdall, which Don eyed suspiciously.

"Oh my God Neil, I hope you're not going to do anything silly, I really am so sorry about everything. Please forgive me. Have you forgotten we are friends?"

Neil stepped forward and for a moment he thought he was going to strike Don, who had instantly scuttled backwards, out of reach.

"Were you mean, don't you*?"* Neil snarled at him. "Don't say the word friend *to me…you little shit! You* don't know the meaning of the word. Now shut up and listen. This is exactly what you are going to do*."*

He opened the holdall, and from it he took a two-gallon plastic container of water, a plastic bowl, soap, a disposable razor, toothbrush and paste, a comb, a towel, and a small plastic mirror.

He pushed Down over towards the drain.

"Now get yourself cleaned up, and then shaved."

Neil had purposely timed this final visit for mid-day when the sun would be directly overhead, lighting up the chamber.

He watched impassively as Don poured water into the bowl, washed himself then shaved, waited until Don had completed his toilet then spoke again.

"Now, put everything back into this," he said, handing Don a large plastic bag.

He took it from him, and put it into the holdall.

"Now get dressed and hurry it up."

Don stood there, now fully dressed in a grey lightweight suit and black shoes, and he was beginning to look almost cheerful, his haggard face now displaying signs of expectation. Neil noted with satisfaction that Don's facial injuries still looked painful.

"Right!" he said. "This is what's going to happen. I've sold your car."

Don began to splutter in protest, but Neil cut him off before he could say anything.

"Just shut up and listen, damn you! With the money, I have paid off your rent for the flat, and bought you a ticket on this afternoon's flight to Cape Town, where everyone thinks you are now. I told everyone at the office that you received an urgent phone call from your father in Cape Town saying your mother was seriously ill, and that you should come at once.

I have approved your application for a months leave. The pay for which you won't get, because after a couple of weeks you are going to write to me, regretfully resigning. You are needed there to help look after your mother, and your holiday pay should be taken in lieu of notice. The rest of your car money is in your inside jacket pocket, together with your passport, and flight ticket.

You will not attempt to contact Fiona. If you do, I will find out; you know I have the money and resources to do it, and I promise you, I will...have no doubt about that, and when I do, I will kill you. Do you understand all of that?"

Everything that Neil had said had been expressed with so much force that Don was in no doubt at all that he meant every word. He gulped and nodded his head.

"Yes I do," he stammered.

Neil picked up the holdall, checked around the chamber to ensure no trace of them ever having been there, and climbed out of the chamber for the last time, with Don close behind.

Don knew better than to try and escape, he followed Neil meekly to the car and climbed up onto the front passenger seat. Neil took a pair of handcuffs that he had bought from an Army Surplus store, clamped one end round Don's left wrist and the other to the metal frame under the seat. Neither men spoke a word on the thirty-minute drive to the airport.

They had time to spare and went through to the cafeteria. Neil bought two coffees and chose a table by itself where they could not be overheard; there were a couple of things he needed to sort out before Don left.

They sat down and Neil took a sip of coffee, he stared into Don's face and said one word.

"*Why*?"

Don tried unsuccessfully to look sad, and at the same time sincere when he answered.

"I love her Neil. I know there were other women. But it was really Fiona I loved."

"And I suppose you think I didn't. Damn it all man, she's my wife, and you were supposed to be my friend. When I think of the times I had you in my home, even getting you to stay there to take care of her when I was away." He took a deep breath before speaking again. "Now, I'm going to ask you a question, and I want the truth, and believe me I will know if you are lying, and if I even *think* you are, you're going straight back to the chamber.

The thought of being underground again made Don go pale and his hands were shaking so much he had to put his cup down.

"What do you want to know?"

Neil hated himself for asking this, but he had to…even though he was dreading what may be the answer. He took another deep breath.

"Did you sleep with Fiona?"

"*What*? No Neil…never…I swear it. Not that I didn't want to, and God knows I tried hard enough to persuade her, but she wouldn't…we never did anything. You must believe me. I think she loves you too much and was really just flirting with me; she seemed

108

upset with you about something, although she never said what...you do believe me don't you?"

Neil looked into Don's eyes, almost daring him to look away. He sighed and slumped in the chair.

"Yes I believe you."

Relief flooded Don's face.

"Thank God for that, thank you Neil."

"There's just one more thing. Who thought up the note in the pipe business?"

Don's jaw dropped.

"How did you...?"

Neil waved his hand impatiently.

"Never mind that, whose idea was it?"

"It was my idea actually, I thought it was quite an ingenious..." his voice tailed off as if realising he was being a bit too glib.

"Just one more thing. How did you know when there was going to be a note waiting for you?"

"Again, that was my idea." He began to smile but stopped when he saw the look on Neil's face.

"Fiona would phone me at the office, but after three rings she would hang up, that's the way I would know."

They had two more cups of coffee, then on hearing the 'last call' for SAA 249 for Cape Town, they went over to the check in desk.

Neil stood with Don as he checked in.

"What about your luggage Sir?" Don was asked.

"It will be on a later flight." Neil told her. She said nothing, but after completing the documentation she gave Neil a funny look.

Don offered his hand to Neil.

"I hope there are no hard feelings, Neil."

Neil stared at him.

"Just get on the plane and go Don, and don't forget what I said about coming back or contacting Fiona. And by the way," he said, waving Don's bunch of keys in front of his face, "I'm sure you would like to know, that when I took your passport from your flat, the lovely old lady that lived next door to you was more than grateful when I told her you were not coming back, and you would like her to have whatever she wanted in there."

109

Neil went up to the viewing area and stood watching as Don walked out with the other passengers and boarded the plane.

His final words to Don had really put the icing on the cake for him. Just to see the expression on Don's face had really finished off what he considered a more than satisfactory ending to a betrayal he would never forgive his one-time friend for.

He stood at the window until the Jumbo was no longer visible before he turned to go home. He took one last look out, to reassure himself his problem had gone, and could not remember when he had last seen the African sky so blue, so clear, and best of all, so empty. Now all he had to do was make sure his marriage could return to the way it once had been in happier times.

Chapter Fourteen

Now, with that little bastard no longer on the scene, eight months had passed. Neil's life had certainly taken a turn for the better, and Fiona was definitely a much happier person. They had resumed their love life as if nothing had happened, and Neil could just imagine the strain she must have been under. But that was all in the past. Maybe sometime when it was right, they would talk about. But then again, maybe not.

He looked at Fiona's face smiling back at him from the photo on his desk and could hardly believe it was three years since it had been taken on their honeymoon on Mahé. He had only been in his office for fifteen minutes, and this was the third or fourth time his eyes had been drawn to it, like a needle to a magnet. Fiona's smile was one of the first things that most people noticed when meeting her, next were her eyes.

One Sunday at the McDonalds, while Fiona and her mother were picking flowers in the garden for Fiona to take home. Neil was flabbergasted, when Duncan suddenly looked up from his newspaper and said.

"Well, my boy, I believe I'm going to be grandfather in seven months time. Well done.

Let's hope it's a boy. Eh!"

Neil just managed to give his father-in-law a sickly grin, at the same time as trying to look pleased. This was news to him, although he had noticed that Fiona was reading books from the library on babies and mentioned several times that this or that friend had either become pregnant, or just given birth.

So that was what the books had been about. She had certainly kept quiet about it. The thought of becoming a father both pleased and frightened him. He remembered the one and only occasion he had actually held a baby; it was the two-week-old son of one his friends.

Fiona had the baby in her arms.

"Here Neil, hold him for a minute." She said, holding the baby out to him.

Neil backed away.

"No Fiona…what if I drop him?"

Then the baby had been placed in his arms; and he stood there as rigid as a lamp post.

"You can move around with him you know Neil,"

He took a slow step forward, and the baby began to slip out of his hands, or at least he thought it was. He panicked and clutched the little bundle to his chest. Somehow the baby must have sensed his uncertainty and began to howl. Fiona rushed over to him.

"Oh for goodness sake Neil…not so *tight*," she hissed at him. "he isn't a bloody rugby ball; give him to me."

Neil had never felt so relieved in all his life as she took the baby from him.

And now just like that, here was his father-in-law, telling him he was going to be getting one of his own.

At seven months, being pregnant certainly agreed with Fiona, and in Neil's eyes, he had watched an already incredibly beautiful woman become even more beautiful; blossoming as an expectant mother.

But that was not to be. Life can be cruel, and early one morning Neil woke slowly from a dream to the sound of moaning, he lay for a few moments thinking it was part of his dream before he realised the sounds were coming from Fiona.

He got out of bed, went round to her side, and switched on the bedside lamp. She had kicked the duvet off, and was lying on her back holding her stomach with both hands, and her eyes were closed. Neil knelt and put his hand on her shoulder.

"What's wrong darling?" he asked, his voice full of concern.

Fiona opened her eyes and looked at him.

"I'm sorry I didn't mean to wake you, it's just that I'm having such dreadful pains…but I'm sure it will pass. Would you make me some warm milk please, and bring me a couple of Paracetamol?"

When Neil returned with the milk and tablets Fiona had moved herself up the bed and was sitting propped up against the headboard. Neil could see a small patch of blood on the bottom sheet and dropped the cup.

"*My God!*" he said, "I'm calling for the ambulance, you're bleeding."

Fiona looked down and saw the blood.

"Don't panic Neil, this sometimes happens."

Neil, who by this time was halfway down the stairs, called back.

"I am not bloody panicking, and you are going to hospital.'

He made his call, and thirty minutes later they were on their way, with Neil sitting opposite her in the ambulance, holding one of her hands and trying to reassure her she would be okay.

The duty doctor examined her and then asked for her to be taken down to the theatre. He then suggested to Neil that it would be a good idea for him to go down to reception and arrange for a private room for Fiona. While Neil was away, he took the opportunity to telephone one of the hospital's gynaecologists and stood waiting for it to be answered; he checked his watch, it showed five thirty.

"Guess who is not going to be the flavour of the month?" he muttered to himself.

After what seemed a lifetime, he heard the phone being picked up, followed by a very sleepy.

"Whoever this is, you had better have a bloody good reason for calling me at this ungodly hour."

"This is Edward Williams. I am sorry to wake you James, but I really could do with your help. I have a lady here…I would guess about seven months on. Her husband brought her in half an hour ago, she woke up with pains around three this morning, and he noticed she was bleeding. We don't seem to be able to stop it, and I really am out of my depth here. I've already alerted the people down at the blood bank, because I have a bad feeling we are going to need them,"

"Sensible of you to call Edward, I'll be there just as quick as I can."

Neil came back from the front desk to find the corridor outside the theatre deserted. He tried looking through one of the windows in the double doors into the theatre, but they were opaque, and he could see nothing. He stood for a while then went along to the waiting room and came back with a chair.

Fifteen minutes later, a tall man with dishevelled grey hair hurried past him, and went into the theatre, before Neil could call out to him.

He was still sitting there, bent over with his head in his hands after an hour, and still no one had come to tell him what was happening. He heard footsteps and stood up. Walking towards him were two women, he could tell by their uniforms, on was a nurse, the other, a ward sister.

"Could someone please tell me how my wife is?" he asked and explained that she had been taken into the theatre ages ago.

"I'm sorry, but we can't interrupt them," the sister said. "As soon as they are able to, someone will be out to see you…in the meantime, would you like a cup of tea or something?"

"Yes please." Neil thanked her and sat down again.

An hour and a half, three teas and a coffee later, the double doors opened with swish, and the front of a gurney appeared, it was being pushed by a theatre orderly, and walking alongside it, now in hospital green was the grey-haired man Neil had seen earlier.

Neil went over and looked at Fiona, she was deathly pale, but the man in green did not appear to be overly concerned so he presumed all was well.

The man spoke to him.

"Are you Mr Owens?"

"Yes. I am. How is she?"

"First let me introduce myself. My name is James Birkenshaw, and I am the senior gynaecologist in the hospital. There is no need for me to tell you that your wife was haemorrhaging quite badly when she was admitted, and when it worsened, the duty doctor quite rightly called me in, and thank God he did. I am dreadfully sorry to have to tell you this, but we were unable to save the baby; in a way, as cruel as it may sound to you at the moment, I think it was probably for the best, although the baby was nearly full term, it was very small, and its chest and lungs hadn't developed compared to the rest of him"…Neil interrupted.

"Excuse me...you said him…him...a boy?"

"Yes Mr Owens it was a boy, but as I was about to say, even had she gone full term, the baby would definitely have died within a month or so. But that is not all I am afraid, I have a bit more bad

115

news, and I think it is better for you to hear this now than later. I am really sorry to tell you that due to complications, your wife will not be able to have children of her own. Believe me I really am dreadfully sorry, but there was nothing else we could do."

By this time, they had reached the lift, and stood waiting for it to arrive. Neil was so shocked on hearing the baby was dead, that for a moment he had forgotten to ask again about Fiona.

"What about my wife, is she alright?"

"Fortunately, yes, we did have a very difficult time stopping the bleeding, and had to give her four pints of blood, she had lost so much. But she will be fine, she is sedated, and I would like her to stay here for a week or so, and then you can take her home. Remember, this has been a terrible ordeal for her, losing a baby this way is a terrible thing for a woman to experience, she will need lots of rest and all the TLC you can give her, especially as this is, I believe, her first pregnancy…I have left you the unpleasant duty to let her know about not being able to have children, but I am sure you will choose the most appropriate time."

Neil assured him he certainly would, and that she would get the best of care.

"I can't thank you enough Sir…I just don't know what I would have done if I had lost her, and I know it may sound callous, but I'm glad, if that is the right word, that the baby died now, rather than later. And you are right, I think it would have been much more difficult for her, after having the baby at home for a while."

"I am glad you see it like that Mr Owens, and I couldn't agree more, just bear in mind her hormones are going to be all over the place for a while, so you will need to be very patient and understanding."

While this conversation was taking place, Fiona with her head spinning, and thinking she was floating on a cloud, could hear a voice she recognised as Neil's, and one other was vaguely familiar. 'Had he just recently been speaking to her?'

With the anaesthetic fogging her brain she could only pick out a word here and there, but the three of them clearly spoken by Neil, were.

"Glad"…"Baby"…"Died," hearing them caused her heart rate to increase with distress. Not realising those three words were totally out of context.

By the time they reached her room, Fiona was fast asleep, with everything she had heard, thankfully erased from her mind.

Neil went down to reception and phoned for a taxi. On the way home, as he sat in the back of the car watching the trees and houses take shape in the light of a new day, he remembered the discussions he and Fiona had had about names for the baby; and after much interference from Moira, they had finally decided on Sarah if it was a girl, and Patrick if it was a boy.

It had taken him a while to accept the fact that he was going to be a father, and over the months had become quite excited about it; but now he was not.

He began to cry softly as the reality of it came to him, their little Patrick was gone, and he had not even seen him. The taxi driver looked up into his rear-view mirror, and on seeing his passenger' distress, discreetly turned the mirror to one side.

Chapter Fifteen

Fiona's parents visited her every evening, and on several occasions when Fiona and Neil were alone, he would notice that her attention was wandering while he as talking to her, and she would look out of the window, her face screwed up in concentration, as if she were trying to remember something.

Aided by Moira, Neil managed to keep Fiona in hospital for a week, and when they finally came to pick her up, her mother told her in no uncertain terms that she and Neil were coming to stay with for a while, saying.

"Neil agrees that it would make much more sense for you to be with us, where you can be looked after properly."

On a Sunday, two weeks after Fiona had left the hospital, little Patrick was laid to rest alongside Neil's parents in the City Park Cemetery. The family had decided to forgo a full church service, with its usual celebration of life, which hardly seemed appropriate, considering that little Patrick had not even had a life.

Duncan had arranged for the vicar who had married Fiona and Neil to hold a small, family only service at the graveside. It was a very difficult service for the vicar to perform, what was there to say about one who has passed away without any of them knowing him?

He quoted a few passages from the bible and said the usual things about only the innocent being taken up to heaven, and God always has a reason.

Neil found it very difficult to accept what the vicar was saying, he knew he was trying to bring them comfort, but there was no way he could understand why the compassionate God he was speaking about should let an innocent baby die.

The weather forecast had been for rain that morning, and heavy black clouds pregnant with rain scudded across the sky, driven along by a brisk wind, interspersed with an occasional patch of clear sky, but the sun was beginning to break through.

Even as the vicar was speaking, blinding rays of sunshine began to lance their way through the gaps in the clouds lighting up patches of the earth, and one ray fell directly onto the tiny white coffin, which was not much bigger than a shoebox, almost as if a sign had been sent from heaven.

Fiona cried out and stumbled, and it was only because of Neil's arm around her waist that she did not fall into the grave, the vicar took this as a sign for him to conclude the service as quickly as possible, without appearing to hurry.

The tiny coffin was lowered into the grave, but neither Neil nor Fiona could bring themselves to throw the traditional handful of earth down on to it. Neil felt that in some way it would be disrespectful. They would leave that task to the grave digger after they had left for home, they did however let a handful of red roses from their garden fall into their son's resting place.

After thanking the vicar, they said goodbye, shook hands, and Fiona, Neil, Duncan, and Moira drove away.

They spent two weeks altogether at the McDonalds, and Neil was able to go to work each day knowing that Fiona was being well cared for. In fact, with two weeks of her mother's cooking, she gained a couple of pounds, and when they returned to Muthaiga, she was looking almost her old self.

Although Fiona looked well, for weeks she was the absolute soul of despair, and no matter what Neil or her parents tried to do, they could not recapture the old Fiona. Moira was especially worried for her daughter, as Fiona was yet to shed a single tear. But time heals all, and six weeks after the funeral, when Neil told her that he wanted to take her to Okavango for a week, which was something she had always wanted to do, Fiona smiled for the first time since Patrick's passing.

Three days later at seven in the morning, Neil took Fiona's breakfast of a boiled egg, toast, and coffee up to their bedroom, where he gently shook her awake.

The previous evening, she had gratefully accepted his offer to pack her suitcase for her and had not complained when he had said they could only take one each. He explained that their luggage allowance was restricted to two suitcases because of limited space on one leg of their journey, and these were already in the boot of the car.

The Okavango Delta in the Northern Kalahari Desert is one of Africa's jewels a natural waterland paradise, measuring just over seven and a half thousand square miles of sweet water, with thousands of islands, some a few feet across, and many of them, hundreds of feet.

They were travelling there using three very different modes of transport. First by light aircraft to a dirt airstrip in Botswana, then twenty miles by Land Rover to the edge of the swamp, and now on the last leg of the journey, in a dugout canoe for the five miles to the small island where their accommodation awaited them.

They had been swiftly gliding along for just over an hour, on open channels of crystal-clear water that separated the islands, some of which were merely clumps of free-floating papyrus, while others were solid land with trees and bushes growing on them, when the silence which was almost palpable was shattered by a long piercing whistle from the man paddling their canoe.

Neil guessed correctly that they must be approaching their destination; the whistle, a warning to someone, of their imminent arrival.

A few minutes later the canoe grounded on a small beach of white sand and they were greeted by an elderly man and woman. They introduced themselves as Joseph and Dorcas, saying they were the caretakers, and that they would be looking after them.

Joseph led them through the trees to their home for the week, a rather primitive looking, but well-built hut of papyrus reeds on a wooden frame, a verandah at the front, topped by a thatched roof.

There was a foot wide gap between the top of the walls and the roof to allow a free passage of air, and the outside appearance belied the inside, where they found everything they would need to make their stay comfortable. The paraffin fridge was well stocked with cool drinks, beer, and milk, and more than enough food.

The warning whistle had given Dorcas just enough time to prepare a tray of fresh coffee, which was now waiting for them on the verandah.

Joseph said they were going back to their quarters; two hundred yards away on the other side of the island, and that they would both return at six to prepare the evening meal, but if they required anything before that, they were just to ring the bell that was suspended from a tree next to the verandah.

After drinking her coffee, Fiona went inside to change out of her travel clothes, leaving Neil to enjoy a second cup. He was studying the flying antics of a hawk lazily circling in the sky above him when he heard Fiona's footsteps. He turned: she was wearing a brightly coloured sarong, which he noticed was fastened at the neck by the pink coral brooch Chantal had brought for her from Mahé.

Fiona reached up with her right hand and gripped the brooch tightly. Her face took on an expression of melancholy, and the simple little bauble somehow was magically transformed from a brooch fashioned from the skeletal remains of long since dead creatures, into the key that unlocked the floodgates of pent-up grief, and she began to cry.

Neil took her in his arms and held her tight, quietly listening, as in between sobs she told him that up until the time she had met Chantal, the thought of having children had never entered her head. But that day she had come to realise how much she wanted a child of her own, she had not mentioned it to Neil, thinking that as he had never spoken about starting a family, he did not want children. And now, a mother was something she could never be. She told him how coming from the operating theatre she had heard him saying he was glad the baby had died.

Neil was horrified on hearing this; he explained about Patrick's condition, and exactly what had been said by himself and Mr Birkenshaw.

Fiona put her hands up and covered her face.

"All this time I have been torturing myself thinking that was how you felt, I am so sorry Neil, how could I have ever thought that. Oh, my darling how you must have suffered as well, and I have never given a thought about that, can you ever forgive me? I've been so selfish, thinking I was the only one in pain."

Neil took her in his arms and shushed her, saying there was nothing to forgive; and that she had never done anything to hurt him.

"Oh, but I have, and I just don't know to explain what I have done." She paused as if to gather strength, and Neil waited, thinking, 'I know what is coming.'

Fiona took a deep breath.

"I've been unfaithful to you!" came out in a rush. "Well, not really unfaithful, as nothing ever happened…it was just a sort of flirtation, because you had upset me and…Oh…all sorts of things. But it really was all pointless and stupid because you didn't know anything about it."

Neil stood up and looked down at her, pretending to be shocked.

"May I ask who with?"

"Well, I did flirt a little with José, but I was meeting another man secretly. But I swear nothing happened between us…although I know he wanted to sleep with me…he told me often enough. But that was not what I wanted. I don't really know what I wanted, I just got caught up in something I didn't know how to get out of.

We used to meet in secret, it was all so mysterious and exciting at first…a schoolgirl sort of thing really. I do love you Neil and I could never sleep with another man. I know I'm not exactly old, but I'm no longer a young girl, and I suppose having another man flattering me turned my head…I am sorry if me telling you this has hurt you, you don't know how long I have wanted to. Can you forgive me?"

"Of course I do you silly girl, and I *do* believe you, but you still haven't told me who the other man was."

Fiona looked at him for a while.

122

"Oh Neil, I know this is going to upset you…it was Don."

Neil turned his back to her, hiding the look of relief on his face. At last he could now put it all behind him. He did have a momentary twinge of guilt as he wondered if he had perhaps gone over the top a bit with Don, after all, Fiona had just verified his story that nothing serious had happened between them; but then the twinge was gone, after all, he had been betrayed by a man pretending to be his friend.

He turned round and put on a look of shock and anger.

"*Right!* That's it then. He went to Cape Town you know, I will be on the first flight tomorrow, and when I find him…goodbye Don Thompson!"

Neil suddenly burst out laughing at the look of horror on Fiona's face.

"I'm joking darling, he's not worth the air fare, and thank you for telling me, I knew something was not right between us, I just didn't know what. Anyway, that is all in the past, we have this island, and the rest of our lives to enjoy."

That night, with their bedroom lit by the flickering light of the paraffin lamp next to their bed, they made love again for the first time in many months.

This outpouring of grief and confession proved to be the turning point for Fiona, her healing had begun, and by the morning of their last day on the island, after time spent in idyllic surroundings with a man who gave her all the love she would ever need, she was almost,   but   not   quite   herself   again.

Chapter Sixteen

As Neil turned into his drive and pulled up at the front of the house, the first thing he noticed was that the whole house was in darkness. He parked the car, got out and stood looking at the unlit windows for a few seconds; something was not right.

Fiona had a thing about lights and switched them all on every evening just before sunset, so by this time the whole place should be lit up like a funfair.

An urgent summons from a pumping station supervisor had taken Neil out of the office just after lunchtime, and he had asked Jean to please phone Fiona, and explain that he should be home by six, but if he was going to be later than that, he would call and let her know; so she wouldn't have gone out.

He called her name from the hall, but there was no reply. He ran up the stairs and went from room to room, he even looked in the wardrobes to see if any of her clothes were missing, but there were no spaces on the racks, it all looked normal. He went downstairs and searched in vain for her.

Now he was beginning to get worried. He stood looking around the room for clues, thinking 'where the hell could she be?' He went into the kitchen to check the pegboard they used for messages. But there was nothing on it except for an old shopping list, and a couple of postcards from friends on holiday overseas. Surely Jean must have given her his message.

Perhaps I should call Jean at home...maybe she has a message for me? Just as he was about to pick up the phone it rang, making him jump. He snatched it up.

"Fiona...?'

It was Duncan, and he sounded concerned.

"Neil, thank God...I've been trying for ages to get hold of you. Can you....?"

Neil brusquely interrupted him.

"Duncan, is Fiona with you?"

"Yes she is....now don't panic son, there really is no cause for alarm, but I think you had better get over here, she's had some really bad news, and she needs you."

"What sort of news Duncan...is it Moira...has something happened to her?

"No, it's not Moira."

"Well let me speak to her. Put her on the phone *damn it.*"

"Neil, calm yourself, she's lying down at the moment, and I think it would be better for you to hear it from her. Just get over here now."

Neil dropped the phone and ran out of the house slamming the front door behind him. He went over the speed limit all the way to the McDonalds, and when he pulled up at the front of the house in a cloud of dust, Duncan was already standing outside the front door waiting for him.

His father-in-law could see that Neil was extremely agitated and took him by the arm.

"Now then laddie, there is nothing at all physically wrong with Fiona, she just couldn't handle the message she got. She's with her mother in our bedroom."

125

Neil rushed through to find Fiona lying on the bed with Moira sitting alongside her. Duncan motioned for his wife to leave the room, and she stood up, saying.

"I think I should…"

Duncan took her arm and gently steered her out of the room.

"And *I* think we should leave them alone for a while, we can speak to them in a minute."

Fiona sat up and clutched at Neil as he sat down on the bed next to her.

"Oh *Neil*, how can we be expected to believe in a loving God when he lets something like this happen?"

Neil had no idea what she meant but had a feeling that she was going to tell him something he really did not want to hear.

"What is it…what has upset you like this darling?"

Fiona let go of him to wipe her eyes and blow her nose. She took one of his hands and began to speak so quietly Neil could hardly hear what she was saying.

"Paul Laporte phoned this afternoon," she paused briefly and began to cry softly before beginning again. "Antoine and his family were involved in a dreadful accident yesterday. They were on their way to spend the weekend at Quelle Fleur; they were forced off the road and down into a ravine by a bus. A doctor was behind them when it happened and saw it all, but there was nothing he could do. Lysianne, Jacque and Marie were killed outright, and Antoine is in intensive care in Victoria…they are really concerned about him."

She had not mentioned Chantal and Neil wondered why, and was just about to ask, when Fiona said.

"Poor little Chantal is in the same hospital, with two broken legs and a few cuts and bruises…she doesn't know about her mother and Jacque and Marie…the poor little mite, I can't bear the thought of her being in pain.

Paul says that Antoine keeps asking for you and wants to know if you will be coming over. They are expecting you to call this evening at the Coco de Mer. Paul and his brother are staying there."

Neil could hardly believe what he had just heard. It was mind numbing to think that three such lovely vibrant people could suddenly be no more.

126

"We'll fly over tomorrow sweetheart…I'm sure it will help Chantal when she sees you again…I'll phone Paul now."

He dialled the hotel number and was lucky to catch Paul just as he was passing the reception desk on his way to the hospital. He was clearly distraught and sounded relieved when Neil told him they would be on the morning flight to Mahé.

"If the flight is fully booked, I'll charter a plane…so don't worry…you tell Antoine we will be there, and that he and Chantal are in our prayers."

Neil called the Kenya Airline's reservation office as soon as they opened the next morning and had a few anxious minutes to wait while the girl rechecked the booking status, after saying the flight was full. When she came back on the line it was to tell him there had been a cancellation, and she was able to offer him two seats. Neil looked up towards the ceiling.

"Thank you God," he said to himself.

To save time he arranged with her for the tickets to be waiting at the departure desk for them. He gave her his details, thanked her, and rang off.

They stayed the night at the McDonalds, and when Neil tucked Fiona up in bed that night, she was much more relaxed than she had been earlier. The thought that she would soon be seeing Chantal, plus three glasses of her father's single malt had seen to that.

Neither of them slept at all on the flight over, with both of them too engrossed in their individual thoughts, worried about Antoine and Chantal's condition, especially Antoine, as Paul had said he was in a very bad way.

Paul must have arranged something with the airport officials at Victoria, because without even looking at their passports they were ushered straight through. When Neil asked about their luggage, Paul reassured him.

"I have someone here who is going to collect it and bring it to the hotel do not worry Monsieur."

On the way to the hospital, he told them the driver of the bus had been drunk and was now in jail.

127

"We have *a* very good punishment here for the people who cause deaths like this, he will be locked away for plenty of years, and will never drive the buses again." He added that the priest had been called to the hospital that morning and had already administered the last rites to Antoine.

Fiona could not hold back her tears when he told them that Chantal was continuously asking for her mother, and that she had smiled for the first time since the accident when she heard that Auntie Feefee was coming to see her.

Neil began to suspect that Fiona was going to be asked if she would break the news to the little girl about her mother and brother and sister.

'Perhaps, it would be better if she was told only of her mother's death first, and then her siblings later,' he thought. But he would leave it to Fiona, she would know what the best way would be to handle it when the time came.

They were both extremely shocked at their first sight of Antoine. His normally tanned face was now deathly pale, his eyes sunken and rimmed with purple bruises. He seemed to be connected to pipes everywhere, and the head of the bed was surrounded by machines beeping and flashing little lights. It did not look at all encouraging.

There was a priest sitting by the bed talking to Antoine, and behind him a tall very sombre looking man. The first thing that came into Neil's mind was, lawyer. He was right. Paul introduced him as Monsieur Hermitte, the family lawyer, Antoine had asked for him to be there.

Antoine tried to smile when he saw his friends. Neil touched the one hand that did not have tubes coming out of it and said hello. There was no point saying how sorry they were about the family; he would know that. Fiona leant over and kissed his cheek.

"Feefee," he whispered weakly, "pauvres petit Chantal."

Fiona was so upset she had to leave the room, after first kissing Antoine's cheek, and asked to be taken to see the little girl.

After she had gone, Monsieur Hermitte turned to Neil.

"Monsieur Owens," he began, "I am here on behalf of Monsieur Laporte to explain his wishes, we do not have much time, and he

128

has asked if you and your wife, as his dearest friends, would take Chantal to be your daughter?"

Neil looked over at the bed to see Antoine smiling at him with a pleading look in his eyes.

"But when he comes...' Neil began. The priest caught his eye and sadly shook his head from side to side. This was one of the thoughts that had been in Neil's mind while on the plane, as a possibility if Antoine died, but he had pushed the thought away. Here and now, it had suddenly become reality.

The lawyer touched Neil's arm lightly to attract his attention.

"All the papers have been drawn up Monsieur, according to Monsieur Laporte's wishes, and have been witnessed and signed", he indicated Paul and the priest by nodding his head at them. "All that is required now, is your approval, and of course your signature."

Neil was stuck for words. Since coming into the room, he had half expected this, but actually hearing it said was still a shock. He looked behind him for Fiona, forgetting that she had gone to see Chantal, he should really speak to her first, but he knew what her answer would be anyway. He could see Antoine's expression was one of expectant hope and made the decision. He stepped over to the bed and took Antoine's hand.

"Of course we will my friend, and we will love her as our own."

Neil signed all the papers M. Hermitte gave him and showed Antoine what he had done.

Antoine was now too weak to speak, and only just managed to give Neil's hand a slight squeeze as tears of gratitude rolled down his cheeks. He smiled at Neil, sighed gently, his hand became limp, and the next moment he quietly passed away.

The machines started beeping and the room was suddenly filled with nursing staff and the four of them were quickly bundled out into the corridor.

The lawyer addressed Neil again.

"There is one more matter Monsieur Owens, Monsieur Laporte also insisted that you and your wife accept the property known as Quelle Fleur with his thanks and blessings, I have the deeds here for you."

129

Neil was at a complete loss for words and was about to protest that they could not accept such a gift, when Paul who had judged his reaction correctly stepped over to him.

"Antoine wanted very much for you to have Quelle Fleur, he knows how much you and your Feefee," he smiled as he said that, "like it so much, and he say you can bring Chantal with you to visit us sometimes…No?"

Neil still could not think of what to say and was glad when the lawyer shook hands with him, saying it was a pity they had to meet under such tragic circumstances and hoped that when Neil next visited Mahé they could perhaps meet for a drink.

Outside in the corridor, on her way to see Chantal, Fiona wiped the tears from her cheeks, not wanting the little girl to see that she had been crying, in case she asked why. She went over to the window overlooking a small park at the rear of the hospital to compose herself and smiled at a small group of children about Chantal's age playing with a little dog. She could faintly hear their cries of joy as they each took turns in throwing a ball for him, wondering who was enjoying it most, them or the dog?

She took a compact out of her handbag and checked her face; seeing Antoine lying there looking so frail and helpless had really upset her, and she just could not stay in the room, her obvious concern for him was definitely something that he should not see.

Satisfied with the way she looked she went to the reception desk and asked for Chantal's room number. The duty nurse smiled at her, on hearing her accent.

"Ah Madame, you must be her Auntie Feefee, everyone who has been in her room since her uncle

said you were coming have been told about you. She is in ward six on the second floor."

Fiona asked about Chantal's injuries, and the nurse explained that she had greenstick fractures in the tibia and fibula of her left leg.

"We were told that she had broken both legs," Fiona said, surprised at that bit of information.

"That is what we thought when she first came in, but the x-rays showed otherwise. She has a few cuts and bruises, but they are minor, she was very lucky, her father was able to tell us that she was lying asleep on the back seat when the accident happened wrapped in a blanket, and fell down onto the floor between the seats, which stopped her from being thrown around. She is doing very well, and seeing you is going to be the best medicine for her, she is very excited, and it has distracted her, she has not asked about her mother for a while now.'

Fiona looked at the nurse, her brow creased with concern.

"I think they are all expecting me to tell her about her family. I just don't know how I will do it."

The nurse smiled in sympathy.

"God will help you."

'He hasn't helped much so far, and just how do you tell a six-year-old that she suddenly has no family?' were Fiona's thoughts as she made her way to Chantal's ward.

Ward six was obviously the children's ward. There were twenty beds in the room, ten on each side and Chantal's was the furthest one away on the left. As Fiona walked down the ward some of the children called out hello to her and she smiled back at them.

Chantal was asleep, lying on top of the bed, looking very peaceful. Fiona sat down on a chair next to the bed and took the opportunity to study the little girl.

There were a couple of scrape marks on one cheek, and two small cuts on her forehead, but apart from the plaster cast on her left leg there appeared to be no other injuries. Fiona gave a sigh of relief; she had expected far worse.

She took Chantal's left hand in hers, and gently stroked the back of it with her thumb, it was so soft, and so small. Chantal's eyes began to flutter and then opened. For a few heartbeats she lay there quite still, just staring up at the ceiling, then she realised someone was holding her hand. She turned her head and her sad little face lit up with joy as she recognised Fiona.

"Oh Auntie Feefee, I am so glad you are here. Have you seen my mama and papa yet? They will be so pleased to see you." She waved one arm around and said in aloud whisper.

"This is a hospital, and all these children they are sick. But the nurse says *I* have been in a car accident. Have you seen my plaster?"

Fiona managed a smile and said yes, and that she wanted to be the first one to write her name on it. She had been really surprised at how well Chantal was speaking, and then remembered that in one of Lysianne's letters she said that Chantal was attending a school run by Nuns, and was having English lessons privately with a retired English ex headmistress.

Chantal's question about her parents had painfully reminded Fiona that sometime the little girl was going to have to be told, but when? Would it be better now, or perhaps later when the memory of the accident had faded a little?

Almost as if she were reading her mind Chantal took Fiona's hand and asked about her parents, and her brother and sister. Fiona's mind went blank, and her heart was aching at the thought of what she had to do, but there was no way they could leave it any longer, with Chantal's questions just being answered with silence or worse, untruths. The little girl had definitely picked up on Fiona's unhappiness and knew something was wrong.

Fiona was just about to speak when she heard someone walking down the ward. She turned and was relieved to see it was Neil, maybe it would be easier with the two of them there. Somewhere along the way he had managed to acquire a large teddy bear with a big red bow round its neck.

He bent over the bed and kissed Chantal.

"Hello my little angel," he said. He put the bear on the bed next to her. "This is Rupert, and he is going to stay here with you, and help you get better quickly, say hello him."

Chantal smiled, picked up the bear and hugged him.

"Hello Rupert, my name is Chantal. Oh, Uncle Neil he is lovely, thank you so much." She turned her face up to him, and he kissed her again.

Chantal lifted the sheet and laid Rupert alongside her. While she was distracted, Neil raised his eyebrows questioningly and nodded at the little girl. Fiona slowly shook her and head and shrugged; clearly indicating to him that she did not know how to break the news.

But crunch time came when Chantal suddenly said.

"Uncle Neil, where are my Mama and Papa?"

Neil sat down on the bed and took one of Chantal's hands in his. A lump came into Fiona's throat as she watched her husband, now in the position she had been in earlier. She knew he was struggling, and guilt overcame her.

She touched his shoulder and said quietly.

"Let me darling."

Neil's shoulders sagged with relief and he stood up.

"Thank you," he whispered as she sat down.

"Chantal", she began, "you know you have been in a bad car accident, don't you?"

The little girl nodded and waited for Fiona to say more.

"Well, my darling, it was a very bad accident, and you were all hurt very much. But your Mama, and Jacques and Marie were hurt so badly that God took them up to heaven to help them." Fiona could tell that Chantal knew exactly what she meant, as she began to weep silently.

"What about Papa, where is he?"

Fiona turned and looked up at Neil, the question in her eyes. Neil's slowly shook his head.

"Your Mama needed Papa to be with her and Jacque and Marie so much that she asked God to bring him to them. Now he has gone to take care of them."

The sight of the little girl trying to hold back her grief was far more distressing to Fiona than if she had burst into tears and screamed. She took Chantal in her arms, rocking her gently and stroking her hair. The ward sister who had been watching from the end of the ward came and joined them at the bedside.

"Now my little one I have something here to help you sleep, and it will take away your pain."

Chantal drank the little cup of pink liquid the sister gave her and said.

"Sister this is Rupert, my Uncle Neil has brought him for me, is it alright if he sleeps here in my bed with me?"

"Of course he can my darling, just make sure he doesn't fall out while you are asleep, tuck him in well." She kissed Chantal, and as she turned, she whispered that Chantal would be asleep in a few minutes, and that they should return in the morning.

133

Children are really amazing Fiona thought, as she watched Chantal wedging Rupert under the blanket; they are emotionally far stronger than we give them credit for, and can cope well with situations that would floor some adults.

The sister was right, in less than five minutes Chantal was fast asleep, her face looking relaxed and peaceful. They both kissed her goodnight and went out to find Paul. As they walked along the corridor Fiona asked Neil where he had managed to get the bear.

"You won't believe this, but I bought it from a kid down in reception who was going home, he wanted twenty rupees for it, because he said it was only a day old. He couldn't have been more than about seven, and he wouldn't budge from his price." He laughed and added, "but it was worth it."

Chapter Seventeen

Fiona was more than happy to find that Paul had arranged for them to stay at the hotel and had managed to get them the Queen of the Night apartment. She noticed on their arrival that the hotel staff were obviously still in shock over the news that Antoine had also died, and the normally lively atmosphere was now one of subdued sadness, even the guests, some of whom had been coming to the hotel for years were affected, and the bars that were usually ringing with laughter and bonhomie were half empty and the conversation hushed.

Once they were in the apartment Neil told Fiona about his talk with M. Hermitte and of Antoine's dying wishes, which were for them to adopt Chanal, and the gift of Quelle Fleur.

For a moment Fiona was absolutely speechless. Neil had known his news would come as a surprise, but he was not quite prepared for her reaction. She jumped up from the settee and flung her arms around his neck.

"Oh darling, I don't know whether to laugh or cry. How soon can we start things going?"

Neil eased her away, so he could look at her.

"I knew exactly what you would want; the paperwork has been completed, and I have already signed it all. We now have a beautiful daughter, and a dream cottage by the sea, but what a tragic way to get them."

That part was just too much for Fiona. She threw her arms around his neck and burst out crying, her tears soaking his shirt front.

"At least they are now tears of happiness," he said to himself as he stroked her hair.

Neil and Fiona visited Chantal three times a day for the next four days, and every day they noticed an improvement. On the third day, when they arrived, she was obviously bursting to tell them something, but at the same time wanting to keep it a secret. However, when the nurse came with a pair of aluminium crutches, she couldn't wait to get out of bed and show them how well she could get along with them. She had already been up and down the ward twice, when the nurse told them that Fiona had spent so much time practicing with the crutches that they had to keep taking them away for fear she would overtire herself.

Her doctor was making his evening rounds while they were there and said that they would be able to take her home the next day, saying.

"She can have the cast off in six weeks." He reached down and patted Chantal's cheek, adding with a smile, "I wish I had more patients like her, she is a courageous little girl."

The next day was the day of the Laporte family's funeral, the service being held at ten a.m. in the Immaculate Conception Cathedral in Victoria.

There were so many people wishing to show their respect, that the priest had to call in an emergency electrician to hastily rig up a loudspeaker system, which would enable the dozens and dozens of people who could not get into the cathedral to follow the service.

Neil said to Fiona that Antoine and his family must really have been exceptionally well thought of; there were lawyers, doctors, government ministers, managers from other hotels and even fishermen from villages along the coast among the mourners; and several local dignitaries stood up to give their eulogies.

Antoine and his family were laid to rest side by side, in their family plot alongside Antoine's mother and father and several generations of Laportes, in a small graveyard on a hill overlooking the ocean at Anse Royale.

The mourners made their way back to the Coco de Mer, where drinks and a buffet were waiting for them, set out on rows and rows of tables on the front lawn.

Fiona and Neil met Paul and his brother Henri's wives for the first time, and they were getting on really well, like everyone else they had met in the islands, despite the circumstances, they were warm and happy people. She mentioned this to Neil.

"If you live in paradise, happiness is the only thing you know." But it was more than that, they all seemed so giving and wanting others to share in their happiness.

Chantal had been discharged from hospital and was now with Fiona and Neil at the hotel. That morning, she was keeping a group of children entertained by showing off her skills with her crutches, and even being gracious enough to let some of them try for themselves.

Later, Fiona was sitting with Chantal in the dining room, waiting for Neil to join them, and noticed that he was deep in conversation at a small table on the front verandah with Paul and Henri, and wondered what could be so important to keep him away from her for so long. She shrugged mentally; no doubt Neil would tell her later.

Nothing would have prepared her for what she was to hear that evening over dinner. She was absolutely speechless when Neil told her that he had bought the Coco de Mer, subject of course to her approval. Apparently, Paul and Henri had told him they had no wish to remain hotel owners, not with Antoine gone, they said they knew nothing about running one.

They told him they both had very lucrative businesses on the north coast, teaching, and taking tourists scuba diving, having decided to give up boat building and fishing. They had decided to put the hotel on the market but were a little concerned that it might be taken up by some big corporation, and just become another stereotype hotel; not the pride of Mahé that Antoine had made it.

He told her they were delighted when Neil told them of his interest, and readily agreed to meet him together with the family lawyer the next day; if Madame Fee Fee was happy with his plan.

Fiona was feeling a little dubious about this new venture and voiced her concern.

"But Neil you know nothing about running a hotel."

"I said I wanted to *buy* it darling, not *run* it, I would get a manager, and if we go ahead with this, we don't even have to look for one, we have one right here almost on our doorstep. A young guy that trained under Antoine for three years is at the moment the manager of a hotel in Mauritius, and he has been just waiting for a chance to come back to Mahé, Paul says he will snap it up. What do you think darling...or do you want to sleep on it?

"Well, I know you have a good head on your shoulders for business, and if that is what you want, then let's go for it." The initial shock had now worn off, and the more she thought about it, the more excited she began to feel; and told him so. "In fact, I think it is a fantastic idea, and I know Antoine would be happy for you...let's do it!"

While Neil had been discussing buying the hotel, the waiters had been keeping Chantal amused, coming to Fiona's table wearing party hats and comic noses, giving her no time to dwell on her family tragedy. Again, Fiona was amazed at the resilience the child was showing, but despite her smiling face if you looked closely, the shadows of sadness were still there, lurking in the back of her eyes.

The highlight of the dinner for Chantal that night, was when the chef came to the table and created a Crêpe Suzette for her; then when he poured on the brandy and lit it, she clapped her hands in glee at the sight of the blue flames flickering on the dish. Fiona's heart nearly broke as Chantal turned to her, and without realizing what she was saying, said.

"Oh, Aunty Fee Fee, isn't it beautiful, Mama would love to see this."

Neil knew Fiona was close to tears and suggested that as soon as Chantal had eaten her crêpe, it would be best if they all went to bed.

With dinner over, Neil picked Chantal up, carried her to the lifts, and by the time they reached their bedroom she was fast asleep.

They put her to bed, still in her day clothes, and with Rupert in her arms left her to sleep the night away.

The next morning while Fiona and Chantal had breakfast in the apartment, Neil went down to speak to Paul and Henri. He found them waiting in the lounge and accepted their offer of coffee. He

138

told them of his and Fiona's decision, and asked if it would be possible to have a look at the hotel books before the lunchtime meeting with the lawyer.

"That is no problem Neil, come, we can go to the office now."

There was no need for Neil to go through all the books and paperwork. Just the first few items were enough to show him that the hotel had been a money-maker almost from the time it had first opened, and Neil could not help a low whistle of surprise when he saw the occupancy rate. He would be the first to admit he knew nothing about running a hotel; but Antoine certainly did; over the last four years he had achieved an incredible rate of 87%.

"I don't need to see more," he told the two brothers, then asked, "what time are you expecting Monsieur Hermitte?"

Paul answered him.

"Twelve thirty he will be here, perhaps we can all have the lunch together Neil, if that is good for you."

Neil told them that would be fine and went back to the apartment. He found Fiona and Chantal sitting on the balcony with Fiona reading Chantal a story from a copy of Alice in Wonderland, which she had bought from the hotel gift shop. The little girl was spellbound with the characters in the book and insisted on Rupert being shown the pictures.

Neil went into the lounge, made himself a coffee, took it out onto the balcony and sat opposite Chantal, just watching her facial expressions change, as she lived the part of the White Rabbit hurrying along. He wondered if he and Fiona fully realised what a tremendous responsibility they were taking on, by agreeing to become Chantal's adoptive parents. There were no doubts in *his* mind about it, and he could not remember the last time he had seen Fiona looking so happy. Maybe this was a blessing for her in disguise, and the memory of Patrick would at last be laid to rest.

"I'm sorry to interrupt you ladies, but I have to see Monsieur Hermitte for lunch, to talk about the hotel, would you like to join us?"

Fiona put her book down.

"No darling, we would only be bored, wouldn't we Chantal? We will have lunch here. I promised Chantal that I would style her hair this afternoon, I'm sure you will be fine without us, see you later."

The meeting was a success and ended with Monsieur Hermitte telling Neil that all the legal documents for the hotel should be ready for signature in two weeks, and that he would contact Paul as soon as they were.

Back at the apartment, he found Fiona and Chantal on the sofa watching television. Fiona was sitting at one end, with Chantal lying along it, cuddling Rupert, with her head resting on Fiona's lap.

The volume was quite loud and neither of them had heard him come in, so he made himself a coffee, and took it out onto the balcony. He turned the sun bed around so he could see Fiona and Chantal, and lay there quietly sipping his coffee, watching them, and trying to sort out what he wanted to say.

As soon as the program ended he went back in, took a chair from the dining table, placed it facing the sofa, switched off the television and sat down.

"Now ladies, we have something to decide. I have a job to go back to go to, so, what are we to do? The papers for Quelle Fleur will not be ready for a couple of weeks. That means you two can either come with to Nairobi me tomorrow, and then we all come back here when the papers are ready for signing, or you stay here and return with me when that is done.

Most of this had been a bit too much for Chantal to understand and was in tears on hearing Fiona say that she wanted to go back with Neil, thinking she was going to be left behind.

Fiona swept Chantal up and held her tightly against her chest.

"Oh no my little poppet," she said, her face pressed tightly against Chantal's. "We will never go anywhere without you…I promise."

Chantal pushed herself gently away from Fiona so she could look at her.

"Can I take Rupert with me Aunty Feefee, will they let him on the aeroplane?"

"Of course they will, don't you worry about it, he is part of our family now," Fiona reassured her.

Later that evening as they looked down at Chantal lying in bed, with a thumb in her mouth, and Rupert clutched tightly against her, Fiona turned to Neil and wrapped her arms around him.

"Oh Neil," she said sadly, "it's such a pity something that has brought such happiness into our lives should be the result of a tragedy." She looked upwards and said in little more than a whisper "We promise you Antoine and Lysianne that we will take care of your little girl and love her always."

Paul had suggested that perhaps it would be less unsettling for Chantal, if when they flew back to Nairobi, only he and his wife came to the airport.

Neil and Fiona both agreed that would the best way to handle it, then when they came back to sign the papers, the family could all get together again for a while.

They made the farewells as short and as painless as possible for Chantal, but they need not have worried, she was so concerned with making sure Rupert was with her all the time, that she had no thoughts for anything else. And when she found out she was to be taken out to the aeroplane in a wheelchair, before anybody else was allowed on board, well, that really made the day for her.

As the plane took off, Chantal pressed Rupert's face up against the window.

"Look Rupert, that's where you were born, now we are going to   a   new   home."

Chapter Eighteen

Duncan picked them up at the airport, and as Neil was getting into the front passenger seat, he nudged Neil's elbow and winked. Neil smiled in acknowledgement; he knew what his father-in-law meant. By telephone from the island, Neil had arranged a little surprise for Fiona and Chantal.

When they turned into the drive, they were confronted by two builder's vans and a lorry with fence poles on it, and Fiona asked Neil what was going on?

"It's a secret darling, just wait till we get in and I will show you."

Once the cases were unloaded and, in the house, Neil took them around the back of the house, but Fiona could see nothing out of the ordinary. She could hear the sound of men's voices, and things being banged around, but was still none the wiser.

"This way everybody," Neil called out as he hoisted Chantal up onto his shoulders Then with her crutches in one hand, he made his way through the garden towards their vacant plot.

Fiona could not believe her eyes. The two-acre plot adjoining their garden, had always been kept as just a field, which Neil's father had planted with grass. Now there was a stable with double doors at the far end, with what was obviously a grain and feed store, almost finished, next to it. There were workmen everywhere, some where digging fence post holes, while others were already putting poles into the ground around the plot.

Duncan turned towards Neil and Fiona with a huge smile on his face.

"They have assured me that it will be finished by late this afternoon, so don't panic."

"Just what is going on here Dad" Fiona asked. "Who arranged all this?"

Duncan explained that Neil had phoned him the week before and asked him to get it all started.

"We were hoping it would be finished before you arrived, but as they've only been at it for four days, I think they have done jolly well.'

"Yes, I suppose they have, but for goodness sake, what is it all for?"

Duncan looked at Neil.

"Don't tell me you haven't told her."

Fiona was beginning to get a little het up, and Neil could see the tell-tale red patches beginning to appear on her cheeks.

"Well, Neil!" she said with her hands on her hips. "Put Chantal down and explain!"

Neil lowered Chantal to the ground and placed her between himself and Fiona. He looked over at Duncan for a bit of support, but Duncan suddenly found that he was needed over at the stables and walked off.

"Thank you very much Duncan," Neil muttered, then smiled at Fiona. "I've bought a pony for" he said, pointing his finger down at Chantal, "it will be here in tomorrow morning."

Fiona felt her anger evaporate as she realised what Neil was trying to do. What a wonderful way to help a child return to normal after having her world turned upside down?

"Oh Neil, what a lovely idea. Chantal, Neil has bought a pony for you, and as soon as your plaster is off, we will teach you to ride."

Chantal seemed a little bewildered by it all and looked from Neil to Fiona before asking.

"My very own pony, does that mean Rupert will be able to ride him as well?"

Neil laughed out loud and picked her up.

"Of course he can poppet. Come on, let's go and have some tea, so the men can get on with their work."

The next morning, the man Duncan had bought the pony from phoned to say they would be arriving in twenty minutes, and when the horse trailer pulled up at the front of the house, Chantal had already been there for ten of them, sitting in a chair with Rupert clutched to her chest.

The driver lowered a ramp at the back of the trailer and then led out the most beautiful little Palomino pony imaginable. Chantal pushed herself up out of the chair and hopped over to it.

"Is it a boy or a girl?" she asked the man holding the pony's halter.

"A girl, and she's pretty, just like you."

Chantal stood with her head to one side, deep in thought.

"Hmmm. I think I will call her Honey, because I like honey, and she is the same colour."

"Honey it is then," Neil said. "Now we will have to get a board with her name on it to go over the stable door."

Almost two weeks to the day, Paul phoned to say the papers were now ready to be signed. But when Neil told Fiona they could now go back to Mahé and finalise the deal, she thought it might be best if he went alone.

"Chantal is settling in so well I honestly think it might be too much of an upheaval again for her. We can take her back for a visit later, Paul will understand, you'll see."

Neil took the morning flight, and by one o' clock the deal was done and dusted. He just managed to catch the afternoon flight home and was delighted to find Fiona, Chantal and Rupert waiting for him at the airport, and went home a happy man; he now had two beautiful ladies who loved him, and a hotel, and a holiday home in the Seychelles.

When the day came for Chantal's plaster cast to be removed, Fiona drove her to the hospital, after phoning Neil asking him if he would meet them afterwards for lunch at the Thorn Tree, which was one of Chantal's favourite places.

Chantal would not let the nurse throw the cast away saying she wanted to take it home with her. Fiona was not happy about it, as after having it on for six weeks, it was a bit smelly, but decided to humour the little girl, and said it was okay, knowing that it would not be too long before it would be forgotten and could be put in the bin.

Neil arrived, and while they were eating, he put a suggestion to Fiona.

"I've been mulling the idea over for a while of perhaps selling my business and moving to Mahé."

Fiona opened her mouth to speak, and Neil put a hand up to stop her.

"Just a second darling, hear me out. I don't intend to run the hotel. That is what the manager is for. I thought perhaps we could live at Quelle Fleur and I could start a deep-sea fishing business, like Guy's. I can think of far worse ways of making a living. I already have a buyer in mind for our business here, for a damn good price. But I want you to think about it, there's no rush."

Fiona smiled at him.

"It sounds great, and you're right, we can think about it, but if we did go, what about?" She looked over at Chantal who was

145

engrossed in her peach melba; our recently acquired four-legged friend?"

"That would be no problem at all, we could fly her out, or we could all go with her by boat," he assured her. "I just wanted to put the idea as a possibility in your mind, that's all."

Neil decided to take the afternoon off and phoned Jean to tell her. Once back at Muthaiga, Chantal wanted to sit on Honey, and waited impatiently while Neil put on her saddle and bridle. She had never been on a horse before, and Neil led her round the paddock a few times before saying he thought she had had enough for the first day.

Over the next few weeks Chantal grew more experienced and confident, until she was able to trot round the paddock by herself. But one morning she was a little too adventurous and shook Honey into a gallop, this proved too much for her, and she slipped from the saddle hitting the ground hard. She lay there without moving.

Fiona screamed and ran over to her, but she was just winded, and as Fiona lifted her up, Chantal noticed the tears on Fiona's cheeks.

"Oh *mama*, please don't cry, I am not hurt."

To Fiona that one word, 'mama,' was the most beautiful word she had ever heard. It meant that at last the little girl had broken free of her pain and had finally accepted Fiona as her mother. Now they could begin to function as a complete family, whatever they decided to do with their future lives; and wherever.

* * * * *

146

Printed in Great Britain
by Amazon

63851869R00093